Aaron Stone: Dancing With the Devil

Kathryn Dawn Samuel

Edited by Courtney A. Karmiller

Revised by Alyssa S. Hodges

Cover Art and Design by David Miller

Please note that all characters, as well as their names and personas, are fictitious in this work.

Dedication

To God, the Creator of the universe. Without You, this book would never be. Thanks for being by my side and guiding me through life.

To my three, wonderful boys, David, Christopher, and Dakota. Thank you for believing in me and encouraging me through this process.

And to my friends, work friends, and loved ones who stood by my side through the ups and downs of writing this book. You motivate me.

Table of Contents

Preface

Only the Devil himself could possess such piercing, red eyes. I couldn't take my own eyes off of them. Everything inside of me desperately wanted to look away. But I wasn't strong enough to resist.

"From the day you were born, you were meant to be mine. No other will have your body or your soul; you belong to me."

His low, deep growl sent shivers rippling down my spine. Fear gripped my entire being. I had never before experienced such an intense presence of evil. Somehow, I found my voice and managed to speak with authority.

"I belong to my Father, the One True God, and nothing can ever separate me from Him." Fire flashed in his eyes. The expression on his face became one of amusement, as though he found himself speaking to an ignorant child.

"You are *mine*, Angela. All will be revealed to you shortly."

I opened my mouth to speak again, but my mouth couldn't seem to form words. Suddenly, I felt myself falling backward...

Aaron Stone: Destiny Awakens

I woke up shivering on a hard table that felt like ice beneath me. The figures that were shrouded in dark robes surrounded me and chanted in unison. They held silver goblets that glimmered in the candlelight cast by tall, black candles on golden stands that encircled the room. Foreign to my six-year-old ears, the words they chanted echoed off of the stone walls.

A strange scent began to fill the air. I would later recognize it as incense. The robed figures slowly raised their silver goblets and light ricocheted in all directions. The chanting grew louder. Feeling suddenly afraid, I wrapped my arms tightly around myself, comforted by the satin of the white dress I'd worn to my baptism several weeks earlier. Wind rushed suddenly through the room as their chanting ended, causing the light to flicker rapidly. An evil foreboding enveloped the room. I squirmed and a whimper escaped from my lips.

"Shhh…Angela, be still. You are honored with the presence of the King of Darkness. Lucifer himself has *chosen* you to become his."

My godfather, Ralph Ackerman, in his thick German accent, whispered the words into my ear as he held my arm down on the table. If the words had not belonged to him, I would not have been obedient. But since my real daddy had passed away unexpectedly from a heart attack, just months earlier, I had begun to trust Ralph like a father. He picked me up on the afternoons when Mommy went to talk to her therapist, Dr. Smith. When Mr. Ralph had picked me up on that particular afternoon, I'd been taking a nap, so I was groggy on the ride to wherever this dreadful place was. I vaguely remembered wondering what was going on as he helped me change into my white dress, but again, I trusted Mr. Ralph.

A man with milky skin had appeared, seemingly out of nowhere, walking towards me as the wind whipped through his long, black hair that was parted down the middle. The starkness of his features made his eyes stand out. They glowed a deep, blood red in the center of his elongated, yellow pupils.

I tried to keep my body still as I began to tremble uncontrollably again. I felt the moisture of my own tears as they rolled down my cheek and dropped onto the silky, white pillow beneath my tiny head. When the man looked down into my eyes, I saw what looked like fire burning in his. It was as though he could see *inside* me with those eyes. I watched as he lifted a hand from underneath his purple robe. There was a ring on his middle finger, with a large blue stone. Sliding the ring off of his hand, he passed it to the robed figure standing beside him. His nails were long and pointy, scratching my flesh as he forcefully placed his hand under

3

my white dress, tracing up and down my cold body. The fingers attached to those long nails found their way into unspoken places where I knew they didn't belong. A warm, tingling sensation coursed through my body as he looked into my eyes. Those eyes glowed even brighter as he growled in a deep voice, "Yes, my Angela. Doesn't that feel good? You are so special. You belong to me and no man will ever have you. You are now mine, forever."

The chanting began to rise again, louder and louder, as the shadows in dark robes drew closer to us. I watched in horror as he slipped his hand out from underneath my dress and licked the blood dripping from his fingertips. I began to scream and cry.

"No! Please go away! I want my mommy! I want to go home! Mr. Ralph! Mr. Ralph!"

Leaning over to press his body hard against mine, the evil man kissed my neck and whispered into my ear, "I love you, little one. You are now mine. Forever."

Taking his ring back from the man beside him, he turned and disappeared into thin air. The chanting continued to grow in volume as they began to walk in a circle around me, holding their silver goblets over their heads, repeating, "Hail to the King of Darkness! Hail to Lucifer! This virgin is your Queen, chosen to accompany you through eternity!"

I had never been so terrified in all of my life. Even at six years old, I had heard of Lucifer. He was also known as Satan, God's enemy. And now, I belonged to him.

In Secret

Mr. Ralph somehow managed to calm me down and the dark figures in robes exited the room. Wiping the tears from my eyes with the sleeve of his robe, he asked, "Why are you crying, Angela? You should be happy, sweetheart. You are now a *princess*. You heard what the Great King said to you. You are special and you will soon be his Queen." I blinked, trying to understand his words. "Angela, a beautiful princess, that's what you are!"

"I can't wait to tell Mommy!" I blurted out. Maybe when Mommy heard that her little girl was a princess and soon to be a Queen, all of her sadness would disappear, just as the man named Lucifer had.

Mr. Ralph smiled back at me as he bent down to pull a blue bag out from underneath the table. Setting the bag down beside me, he unzipped it as pulled out my pink sundress and matching pink flip-flops.

"Angela," he explained softly, "we can't tell Mommy or anybody else about this. Mommy might get mad at me for bringing you here. This is our secret, okay?"

"Okay, Mr. Ralph. I don't want Mommy to get mad."

As I got cleaned up and dressed, I kept thinking, *I'm a princess, soon to be a Queen*, but it did little to numb the stings I felt from the scratches.

"Ouch," I yelped. "It hurts…that hurts!"

Mr. Ralph made a clicking sound with his tongue, trying to distract from the pain.

"I know it hurts, sweetheart," he answered back. "We will tell Mommy we were playing frisbee in the park and you ran into a sticker bush to catch it."

"Okay." I nodded my head, but felt slightly guilty about the fact that we were planning to lie to my Mommy. Once I was dressed, Mr. Ralph helped me down off of the table.

"Are you hungry, my little princess? How about a hamburger at Burger Town? Maybe followed by some ice cream?"

"Yes, yes, yes!" I jumped in anticipation.

* * * *

From then on, Mr. Ralph referred to me as "The Little Princess." He brought me lots of princess toys. One of my favorites was a beautiful crown. On the inside, it said, "To a Beautiful Princess and Future Queen of the World." We never mentioned a word to my mother about what happened that day. Life went on as if nothing had ever happened, but I knew inside that the day was coming when I would be the Queen. And then, Mommy would be happy.

At night, I had nightmares about that man, Lucifer. I would picture his face and his burning red eyes as he touched my body over and over again. I'd wake up, scared to death, but I didn't dare tell my Mommy about my nightmares. If she found out what had happened, she wouldn't let Mr. Ralph come around and there would be no more princess toys.

My First Encounter with the "Antichrist"

I never forgot those piercing red eyes, which is why I recognized them when I saw them again. It was a busy night at the restaurant; guests were lined up outside the front door, waiting for a table in our Asian fusion, high-end lounge. Romance was in the air; reflections of lit torches flickered in the waters of the infinity pool surrounding our gorgeous outdoor patio. I can still hear the jazz band playing softly, and I recall the glow of the full moon against the dark night sky.

Our four-star restaurant attracts a plethora of celebrities and high-profile personalities, but when I caught a glimpse of Mr. Aaron Stone that night, it caught me off guard. He slipped in through the side door with his business partner, Billy. They seated themselves at one of the high top, marble tables in the bar. Although they were deep in conversation, I could feel Aaron staring at me. As I greeted guests and walked them to their seats, he watched my every move—or so it seemed to me. I suppose I could have just been paranoid, but I felt his bright, unnaturally blue eyes following me. When I finally threw a glance in his direction, I saw his eyes *glowing* that same piercing red. Looking away quickly, a million questions swam through my head.

Oh my God, am I going nuts or did I really just see that? I assured myself that I was probably so busy that my mind was playing tricks on me.

A strange feeling washed over me; it was an overwhelming aching, as if I was burning with a fever. My body started to tremble, and a high-pitched ringing filled my ears. Something had happened after that glimpse of his eyes. I felt the same weakness I had experienced when I'd had that dream. My thoughts became scattered and I struggled to focus. It was as if Aaron had taken control of me with his eyes in that brief moment.

* * * *

It was not until early summer that I finally came face-to-face with the man who claimed to be inhabited by the Devil himself, and claimed to be the Antichrist. I had been working at the restaurant for quite some time; it had almost become my second home. My son Nicholas, "Nick" for short, had become one of the bartenders, which was perfect for his friendly personality. On this particular night, as the restaurant was slowing down, Nick motioned me over toward the bar. I felt Aaron's eyes follow my steps as I passed his table.

"Ma, I want you to meet one of my regulars," Nick explained in his thick, New York accent, "Aaron Stone."

I hadn't felt or heard Aaron's movements, but he was suddenly beside me, reaching out to shake my hand. His grip felt magnetizing, like an electric shock running through my body. Instinctively, I knew this man was dangerous, yet I felt drawn to him somehow.

"It's nice to meet you," I heard myself say, but my eyes did not meet his. I was afraid his gaze would entrance me. In the reflection of the glass, I noticed a couple entering the front of the restaurant. Without waiting for his response, I pulled my hand away from his and walked back over to the hostess stand to greet them.

Several weeks later, I received a startling email from my ex-husband. Although we had recently divorced after fourteen years of marriage, Kyle and I continued to communicate frequently on amicable terms. The subject of the email was: "Aaron Stone." In the email, Kyle explained that Nick had been telling him some strange stories about the mysterious man who called himself Aaron Stone and Kyle had become deeply concerned. Kyle explained he had done some digging online and discovered that there was much more to Aaron Stone than what met the eye.

According to Kyle, the Stone family had ties to royal blood, but little was known about Aaron himself. After stumbling upon a thread in a secret society's forum, Kyle concluded that Aaron Stone was merely a delusional imposter and a con artist. *There is reason to believe that Aaron Stone sees himself as Lucifer incarnate, waiting in the wings to step in as the Antichrist when the New World Order is brought about*, Kyle wrote. *Angela, I know you believe in what*

Revelation says about the End Times. Whether Aaron's body is inhabited by the Devil or not, from all of the research I've done, he will become the Antichrist.

Kyle had attached several of the documents he'd found, as well as the thread that had concerned him the most. I skimmed through each attachment, wondering how accurate such third party information could really be.

The email also contained a warning: Kyle instructed me to keep our son away from the man and to ensure that he would never set foot in our home. While I had not yet entirely cast judgment on the mental well being of the acquaintance in question, Kyle's words sent chills creeping up my spine. The information Kyle had found made it crystal clear that Aaron Stone believed himself to be Lucifer redeemed, the so-called 'Antichrist,' come back to Earth.

Fear for my son began to consume my dreams. I woke up from nightmares in a cold sweat. Part of me believed the things that Kyle said and knew I had to protect Nick, but another part of me needed to find out the truth for my own sake. I wanted answers and the only way to find them would be to approach Aaron himself. I needed to know who he really was—and, more importantly, what he wanted from my son.

As though he could read my mind, he made an appearance at the restaurant the very next day. As I walked toward him, I felt my heart beginning to pound. I felt inexplicably terrified. But I reassured myself with what I hoped was the simple truth: *He's not evil; he's*

11

insane. I approached the man who had bestowed so many strange titles upon himself and got straight to the point.

"Who are you *really* and what do you want with my son?"

The first words Aaron ever spoke to me were: "Would you like to sit down and let me buy you a drink?"

The timbre of his voice was distinguished and his invitation was polite. Every dark hair on his head was perfectly in place and the scent of his cologne was enticing. Aaron Stone didn't even blink, regarding me as though he hadn't even heard my words. If my memory served me correctly, his eyes had been a brilliant blue, but those eyes that held mine directly in his gaze were piercingly green. All of the colors that surrounded us seemed to mute in comparison to those eyes.

"No, thank you," I said finally. "I know the claims you make. Eternity is forever and God is not to be mocked." Unsure of where my words came from, I walked away, shaking with each step. It was frustrating to find myself more puzzled by the brief exchange than I had been when I approached him. At least I had my job to distract me from the mysterious stranger. For now.

As I watched as a happy couple in a sleek sports car whip into the restaurant's parking lot, I thought of Kyle. Memories came rushing back in waves…the exciting places we had been together, the sweet things we had promised each other. It was heart wrenching to watch Kyle pack his bags and walk out the door, taking with him the last fourteen years we'd shared and the future we'd planned.

The walls of depression had started to close in on me. Fear and loneliness consumed me. I knew that all I needed was to find a few friends—good friends. Aaron Stone was not the kind of friend that I was looking for, nor was he the kind that I needed in my life at the time. But still, there he was sitting in the bar, watching me as if he was instinctively aware of my desperation and despair. Aaron seemed to know right where to find me, how to speak to me, how to pique my curiosity. I had wandered into the lion's den without even realizing it.

I have always been a spiritual warfare advocate, so the sensations I experienced every time Aaron was around made me wonder—*Am I now being tested on the very thing I preach?* I constantly sought out the signs of God's divinity in my life. The strange things I noticed, things some might refer to as "coincidence," were like intricate pieces of a big picture puzzle to me.

These events began with a photo. I decided to take a different route to the mall and noticed a picturesque little church just off of the side of the road. I felt strangely compelled to stop and photograph the church. After pulling over, I slid my phone out of my purse and snapped a shot of it. Getting back onto the road, I put my phone away and thought nothing of the picture for several months.

I began to attend a church that offered a divorce class. I met a woman in the class named Alyssa who encouraged me to visit a labyrinth where she went to pray and meditate.

"Alyssa, what is a labyrinth?" I had heard the term, but wasn't sure what it meant.

"It's a maze of footpaths that lead to a central area. As you walk on these paths, you pray through your worries. When you reach the center, you wait for God to speak to you."

As odd as it sounded, I guess I was at a point in my grief where I would have done anything to understand the pain I was feeling, so I decided it was worth a try. As soon as I arrived at the address Alyssa had given me, it hit me—this was the same church I had snapped a photo of nearly a year earlier. Around the back of the tiny church, vines climbed the fences that surrounded the labyrinth.

As I walked the winding footpaths of the labyrinth, I prayed silently. The paths started to confuse me after a while. They were not straight; they kept leading me back to where I began. Terribly frustrated and feeling trapped in a twisted metaphor of my own life, I prayed. *God, I am trying to get to You, but I can't find the path that leads to You!* I remember tears filling my eyes as I thought, *My life is in shambles and I can't even get to the center of this labyrinth!* I became more confused by the second, but all of a sudden, I heard a soft, still voice say to me, *"I am here, Angela; come to Me! Just step to your left and walk straight. Come to me, Angela."*

I wanted to give up, but that small voice encouraged me to keep going, melting away my frustration. *I can do this*! I told myself to be patient and to trust the voice. *You can't give up; you will make it to the center. It might take time, but use that time to pray and stay focused.*

"Angela, Angela! These people need to be seated! Snap back, missy! What were you thinking about?" An irritated voice pulled me back to reality.

"Life," I replied, laughing it off. But the truth was, I was having trouble staying focused. Minutes slowly ticked by as I waited for my shift to end. As soon as it was over, I headed out the side door to my car. I looked up and there he was, standing right in front of me, smoking a cigarette. This time, I looked straight into Aaron's face. Even though I can't recall one damn word I said to him, I do remember feeling fear mingled with a strong attraction.

What am I doing? I chided myself inwardly. *Am I losing my mind? Why am I even entertaining the thought of having a conversation with this freak?*

Kyle's email should have made me wary. Aaron claimed to be the Antichrist. Apparently I hadn't gotten my point across when I approached him that day because he was lingering. *If he thinks we're going to have a friendly little chat, he's dead wrong.*

I knew I had to get away from him fast, so I just ignored him and kept walking. As I got into my car, a startling thought found its way into my mind. *Do you feel attracted to him, Angela? Could it just be the loneliness after the separation? Has it really been two years already?* A disturbing thought emerged. *If he really is the Antichrist, maybe Lucifer is using Aaron to hypnotize you, Angela.* I shook my head as if it could make that idea go away.

I took one last look at Aaron. Whoever he really was, all I knew was that I had to stay away from him. I started my car and drove out of the parking lot without another glance.

August 12, 2010
Falling Fast

On my way home, I felt paranoid. I constantly checked my rearview mirror to make sure Aaron Stone wasn't following me.

"Come on, Angela," I chided myself out loud, trying to shake it off. "This is nuts."

I decided to stop at the drugstore to pick up a birthday card for my sister. A homeless man who was sitting on a bench near the parking lot caught my attention.

"Ma'am, could I trouble you for some change?" The man looked like he hadn't eaten in several days. I dug around in my purse, but all I had were a couple of quarters.

"Here," I said, dropping the quarters into the Styrofoam coffee cup he held, "I'm sorry, I don't have anything else with me." His eyes were bright as he smiled up at me.

"Thank you. May I give you a word from the Lord in return?" I almost chuckled aloud. A poor, homeless man selling prophesies for fifty cents at the local drugstore.

"Sure," I replied. "Why not?" *This ought to be good.*

"The Lord has asked me to warn you: stay away from the man with the piercing eyes, Angela. He is who he claims to be. Lucifer has possession of his body and he will be enthroned as the leader of the world. He is the one prophesied to be the Antichrist."

My stomach dropped. He knew my name. And he knew about Aaron Stone.

"How do you…? That's impossible," I managed.

"These are the words of the Lord."

I took a few steps back, unwilling to take my eyes off of the man. "Who are you?" I demanded.

"I am a messenger, a courier of peace. May our Lord God protect you, Angela." I was so freaked out I forgot about my sister's birthday card and quickly turned to climb back into my car. As I pulled out of the parking lot, I glanced back over at the bench. The homeless man had disappeared. I didn't feel safe until I had driven straight home and bolted the lock on my door behind me.

About two weeks later, my friend Kristine and I decided to grab dinner after a mid-week church service. We chose a vibrant little Mexican restaurant near our homes. This place was known for its spacious outdoor patio. It was a gorgeous evening—not too hot, not too cold, and the sun was just on the verge of setting. We chose the only open table outside. It was near the center, in between tables where other customers chatted happily as they sipped their margaritas and the smell of spices filled the air.

As we sat waiting for our server, I absentmindedly glanced around for familiar faces—*Aaron Stone is here!* There he was, midway through his dinner, sitting with my friend, Bob. *Why is Bob with him?* Bob and I had been introduced at the restaurant a few weeks earlier. Bob was a songwriter; but then, in Nashville, who isn't?

Aaron leaned across the table and said something to Bob, who turned and noticed us. Bob approached our table and asked if he and Aaron could join us. I would have said no, but before I could get a word out, Kristine blurted, "Yeah, sure, come on."

As they walked over, I could feel Aaron Stone's eyes boring into me behind his dark sunglasses. Of course he had to choose the seat directly across from me. I immediately felt my heart begin to pound. *There is something so strange about this man. Why do I feel so weak, so anxious around him?* I needed a drink to calm my nerves—and I needed it right away.

After two drinks, an appetizer, and an entree, Bob invited us to his house. Again, I should have declined, but acquiescence prevailed before I could think twice. As soon as we walked through the door of Bob's house, Aaron picked up one of Bob's guitars and began strumming a beautiful melody. As we all listened intently, the irony was not lost on me. My friends and I were spending a wonderful evening with a man I had tongue-lashed a few weeks prior because of a warning from my ex-husband. I did not want to like Aaron, yet I felt drawn to him. I had to think of Nick. Whatever feelings I was having toward Aaron, instinctively I knew that I did not want my son to associate with him. *Maybe I am simply attracted to the mystery I see in Aaron. Am I feeling this way because Kyle told me to stay away from him?*

I was a faithful wife all through those fourteen years of marriage. I never entertained the thought of being with anyone else. I loved my husband. I can still remember feeling butterflies in my stomach when he walked into a room. Obviously he couldn't say the same. Free will rules and after he followed his, I began to follow mine. After so many years of building my life around my beliefs, teaching prayer groups and attending Bible studies, something inside of me began to rebel. I had prayed for God to change my husband's heart and He hadn't, so my own heart changed. Perhaps in feeling abandoned by God, I abandoned Him. Either way, I found myself toying with the idea of accepting the advances of someone who claimed to be Lucifer incarnate, the Antichrist.

The music had mesmerized me. I snapped out of my stupor when Aaron slid next to me on the sofa. He whispered into my ear, "Everything you've heard about me is true." It was as though Aaron Stone could read my mind. *What if Aaron is the devil? Does the devil have free will, or is he just a created being fulfilling his destiny? What if the devil repented and asked God for forgiveness? Would God forgive him?*

The most dangerous idea implanted itself in my brain. What if *I* was destined to save the devil's soul?

August 28, 2010
An Evening with Aaron Stone

Aaron Stone managed to break through the walls I built after the divorce. For two years, I refused to allow myself to get close to anyone. But the cool confidence in his voice and the directness of his gaze melted me. Whatever power Aaron Stone had over me, regardless of the source, was irresistible.

One night shortly after the evening at Bob's, Aaron paused at entrance of the restaurant, allowing his colleagues to pass by.

"Angela." The way he said my name made me weak in the knees. "There will be a limousine parked in front of your house in two hours. I will be waiting for you. I am certain you will look ravishing."

With no hesitation, I scribbled my address on a slip of paper and handed it to him.

"Thank you, Angela," he said graciously as he tucked it into his pocket. He didn't even glance at what I had written. "But I always know where you are," he added with a wink.

Although his words should have terrified me, I found myself feeling strangely flattered. As I watched him exit, I realized I could not wait to hurry home and get myself ready for whatever my evening with Aaron Stone held.

What to wear was not a difficult choice. I slipped into a little black dress that hugged my curves in all the right places and reached for my stilettos. As I selected black fishnet stockings I had never had the guts to actually wear, a startling revelation came to me. I was Aaron's prey, caught in the trap he'd set for me. But I didn't panic. Somehow, I *wanted* to be there. I was past the point of mere curiosity. I was hooked.

Once I'd finished freshening my makeup, dabbed on a splash of my favorite perfume, and glanced out the window. There it was— a long, black limousine parked just beneath the streetlight. As I walked down my driveway, the driver stepped out and opened the door for me. The stillness of the night air and the radiance of the moon's glowing halo seemed to make time stand still. My steps slowed and my eyes fell to the ground. I was hesitating.

Free will, Angela. Do you want to dance with the devil in the pale moonlight? Aaron Stone's piercing green eyes met mine when I looked back up. As we stood with our gazes locked, a disarming smile spread slowly over his handsome features. He held out his soft, warm hand to help me in. An electric chill surged through my body as I accepted his outstretched hand. "Hello, Angela, you look absolutely stunning."

"Well, thank you," I replied, blushing a bit as I sank into the black leather seat.

The limousine stopped at an exclusive club near downtown. As we entered, Aaron's countenance changed completely. He shook hands with a man in a custom, pinstriped suit and whispered into a cocktail waitress's ear. It was as if he'd suddenly forgotten I was there. I noticed that even as he flirted with women at the bar, his eyes were on me.

Is this some kind of game? I wondered. I didn't do *games*. Just as I was about to call a cab to leave, he was instantaneously at my side, charming as ever.

"Shall we order a bottle of champagne, Angela?"

Hours disappeared when I was with Aaron. His sense of humor was intellectual, but far from dry. *Damn, I almost forgot how good it feels to laugh*, I thought to myself. I glanced down at my phone and noticed the time. I knew I needed to go home.

All I could think about as the limo took us back to my house was how I would rather be anywhere but there. The thought of that lonely house filled with nothing but aching memories awaiting my return was unbearable.

Always the gentlemen, Aaron Stone guided me to my front door and waited patiently as I unlocked it.

"Goodnight, my Angela," he said softly as his lips brushed my cheek.

"Goodnight," I replied and slipped inside, locking the door behind me.

* * * *

That night, I couldn't sleep. Starlight invaded the spaces between my blinds and no matter what I did, I felt chilled down to my bones.

Frightening thoughts battled for my mind. If there was any chance that Aaron really was the Antichrist, I was putting myself at risk by associating with a man who was controlled by Lucifer. All I really knew for sure was that I claimed to be a child of God and this man's claims threatened everything I stood for.

Once I finally drifted off to sleep, Aaron's eyes haunted my dream. But I had no idea that my reality was about to become much worse than any nightmare I had ever had.

September 3, 2010
The White BMW

A few weeks passed by without Aaron coming into the restaurant, which was fine with me. I was content to fall back into my routine of working and occasionally spending time with friends. Part of me was glad that Aaron Stone seemed to drift out of my life.

One afternoon, when I was feeling lonely and bored, I received a much-needed call from my girlfriend, Marie.

"Angela, there's this new little bar down the road from my house that just opened up. Let's go grab a few drinks tonight."

Marie was a few years younger than myself, but she was mature beyond her years. At 5'3", she was a cute little thing, with a waist that was a bit on the thicker side, long brunette hair, a petite nose that flaunted a hoop ring, and a pair of big, chocolate-brown, Italian eyes. She was adventurous and so much fun to be around.

When we pulled up to the makeshift parking lot of the bar, we could hear laughter echo from the back. The entrance was reminiscent of walking into a big barn. It was dark and smoky, with music blaring from several speakers. We fought our way through the dancing crowd to the bar top. After ordering our first round of drinks, we found our way through one of the two gigantic garage doors that led us outside. The concrete patio in the back was scattered with picnic tables. Most of them were full. The crowd was diverse in age and background, but one thing was clear: every person present was there for the drinks and casual conversation.

As we found a spot at a table, I took a deep breath. The cool air was literally a breath of fresh air. *There's nothing like a crisp chill in the air on a beautiful September night*, I thought to myself. After a couple hours of conversation and a few drinks, we both began to feel tired. I knew it was time to head home. I asked Marie if she wanted to come stay at my house, but she'd noticed a friend who had walked out onto the patio, so she opted to stay and chat.

After finding my way back through the crowd, I jumped into my car and drove out of the parking lot. *The rest of this lonely night is bound to follow suit with all the others*, I told myself. A beep startled me awake at a little past five in the morning. I glanced at my phone on the table next to my bed. It said: *Message Received from Aaron Stone*. I read the text through bleary eyes: 'Do you know anyone who drives a white BMW?'

Fear immediately flashed through my body. Marie drove a white BMW. *Oh my goodness, what happened to Marie?* I began to fear the worst. Before I could respond, my phone beeped again with another text.

'Your friend was pulled over last night leaving the bar. DUI, I believe. Did she call you?'

No way! I jumped out of bed, wiping the sleep from my eyes, and typed my response.

'Explain to me how you would know what happened last night...Or should I say this morning?'

His response came no less than a second later.

'Meet me for breakfast and I will tell you the whole story.'

'The Green House. Is that okay with you?' I typed back.

'Sure, see you in 30 minutes.'

As I rushed to get ready to meet him, my mind raced with questions. *Why didn't Marie call me if she was in trouble? Why did he text me? How did he know what happened to Marie?* Despite the concern I was feeling for Marie, I was glad to find that it was a beautiful morning outside. The sun was shining and the air was humidity-free for once.

It had been a few weeks since I had seen or even spoken to Aaron. I began to feel anxious as I whipped my silver Audi A4 into one of the Green House's few remaining parking spots. I jumped right out of the car, feeling adrenaline rush through my body. *Not again. My heart is starting to race. It's just nerves. Why does Aaron make me feel this way?*

I walked into the restaurant and immediately spied him sitting in a booth, still wearing his dark sunglasses and the same black hat he occasionally wore when he visited our restaurant. As I approached him, I felt a strange—almost electrifying—feeling wash over me.

I folded myself into the booth across from him, noticing his leg brush mine under the table. A warm sensation ran through my body. *Hurry up! Say something, Angela! Don't get distracted. This is about Marie, not Aaron.*

"What happened last night?" I asked without bothering with pleasant greetings.

"Are you hungry, Angela?" Aaron had a way of pretending not to hear my questions, which I did not appreciate one bit.

"I am hungry and I could use a cup of coffee to wake up, but I really need to know what happened to my friend, Aaron."

Part of me wanted to hurry the conversation up so I could get the hell out of there. Another part of me was studying him—the features of his face, the clothes he wore, the tattoos on his folded hands, which appeared to be some sort of Egyptian writing, maybe Hieroglyphics.

"They're symbols for the sun and the moon," Aaron said gently, reading my thoughts.

Before I could respond, he cleared his throat. "Why don't you glance at the menu and I will explain once you've ordered something for breakfast?" I quickly perused the menu and when the waitress came, I ordered coffee and an omelet. Aaron followed suit.

"So, tell me what happened. And how it is that you are aware of last night's events," I said firmly, refusing to allow him to stall any longer.

"I arrived with my friend, David, just before you left Marie. We were drinking on the patio and noticed you and Marie, but I did not want to disturb your conversation. After you'd gone, Marie began chatting with a few guys. It must have been around 2am when they gave last call. As David and I were leaving, I saw a police car parked just down the street from the bar. I told everyone around us that I was calling a few cabs so we could all avoid driving. Marie insisted that she was fine to drive, saying that she would just follow her friends' cab so she wouldn't have to leave her car at the bar overnight."

"Were you and David taking a cab with her friends?

"No, we weren't. Her friends' cab was right behind ours."

"Oh. Okay, gotcha. Please continue."

"Along the way, our cab came upon an accident. When our driver pulled over to wait for the police to flag him by, one of the police officers walked up to our cab and then the cab behind us, the one Marie's friends were in. When he approached Marie's car, he appeared to ask her to step out of her vehicle. The next thing I knew, Marie was doing a sobriety test. The rest is history, I guess."

"Damn, that really sucks!" I said.

"Yeah, it did for her," Aaron blurted out with a devious laugh. His laugh, and the fact that it was at Marie's expense, made me uncomfortable.

To my relief, the waitress arrived with our breakfast. As I picked at my omelet and sipped my coffee, my mind reverted to all of the questions I had about Aaron after reading Kyle's email. I didn't want to ask any of them; I was afraid to open that door. I decided that small talk was the best way out.

After we'd finished eating, Aaron paid the bill and walked me out to my car.

"Angela, what are your plans for the day? Would you like to spend some more time together?"

"Thanks for the offer, but I have to be at work in two hours," I declined.

"Okay, well, maybe another time."

"Yeah, sure," I replied.

Starting my car, I actually found myself thanking God that I had to go to work. I wondered what would have happened if I had gone with him. Fear and intrigue mixed in the unknown.

September 13, 2010
Piranha 3D

Ten days later, Aaron Stone woke me up in the wee hours of the morning again with a text. He was in New York City on business, but would be back in Nashville that evening. He wondered if I would join him for a drink. 'Just text me when you're back in town,' I replied.

At work that night, sometime after the dinner rush, I heard my text tone go off. 'Hey, my flight just landed. Meet me at The Blue Roof at 9 p.m. I would also like to take you to a movie later, if that's alright with you.'

I probably should have come up with an excuse as to why I couldn't meet him that night. But something inside me was ready to face Kyle's accusations about Aaron Stone. I had to find out the truth behind all those crazy claims of Aaron being Lucifer. I wanted—and needed—answers.

I arrived at The Blue Roof a little before nine that evening, wearing a sleek, black sundress with a pair of sexy heels that added three inches to my height. My long, brown hair felt silky against my

31

skin. No matter how nervous I felt, I was always confident about my appearance. My mother always called me a 'mutt' because I'm a mixture of several heritages, but I'm grateful to my Italian ancestors for my brown eyes and full lips.

Aaron was sitting at the end of the bar drinking a martini when I walked through the door. *Damn, he does look good dressed all in black*, I admitted to myself, taking the open seat next to him. His eye caught mine and he leaned over to brush my hair back from my face.

"Would you like a drink?" he whispered into my ear.

"I would like a glass of Chardonnay, please," I replied without hesitation.

"Get the lady a glass of Chardonnay," he winked at the bartender. We fell into casual conversation as we sipped our drinks.

"Piranha 3D," he said, just as I was about to ask one of my burning questions.

"What is Piranha 3D?"

"That's the movie we are seeing tonight, Love."

"Oh, okay," I chuckled. "When does it start?"

"In about twenty minutes—so drink up."

I guess my questions will have to wait. In truth, I think I was relieved that I didn't have to bring up the strange information Kyle had sent me. As I watched Aaron's movements, doubt grew inside of me. Kyle had to be wrong. Sure, Aaron was eccentric, but that was part of his charm. Besides, I didn't want Kyle ruining whatever was happening between Aaron and myself. I decided to let my fears go. Time would tell.

As with most late night movies, the theatre was empty when we walked in. "Where shall we sit?" Aaron asked. "We have the entire theater to ourselves."

We selected seats near the center of the theatre. The girl at the counter had given each of us a pair of ridiculous-looking 3D glasses. I relaxed as we watched the commercials, which looked odd without the glasses, but when the house lights went low and the previews began, I felt Aaron wrap his arm around me. In the dark, his hand slid slowly up my dress. As he started rubbing my thigh, I shut my eyes.

Now what are you going to do, Angela? a voice inside of me asked. I felt paralyzed. Aaron whispered in my ear, "You know, Angela, I would love to fulfill your deepest desires." I was completely vulnerable and he knew it. "Give me all of you, Angela." I felt his hand on the back of my neck. He pulled my hair back and began to lightly kiss my neck. "I can give you pleasure you have never felt before if you open yourself to me. I want you to let me into your soul."

My body began to tremble. *What is he doing?* I had never felt the sensations I was feeling before in my life. I weakly fought against them. *Regroup, Angela, keep cool.* Whatever he was doing, I won't deny that it felt *good.* Desire enveloped me.

All of a sudden, he pulled away and sank back against his seat as though he had been caught and was attempting to look innocent. "I think I am going to have a smoke."

"What? Right here?" I asked, incredulous. "We are in a theater; there are 'no smoking' signs *everywhere*."

"Um, look around us, Angela. We're alone."

Reaching into his pocket, he pulled out a pack of Camel Lights and the flame from his lighter illuminated the seats in front of us. He nonchalantly took a few short puffs from his cigarette. *What is going on?* I thought to myself. *One second he's Prince Charming and the next he's smoking in an empty theater. He's manipulating me with these sick games and I know it, but I can't break free.*

The truth was even worse. I didn't *want* to break free. For the first time in a long time, I felt excitement, flattery, and lust. I felt them more intensely than I ever had with Kyle.

The movie began and I pulled the glasses over my eyes while Aaron put out his cigarette. Whatever the power was that Aaron had over me, I knew I needed help. *The devil is a deceiver. God, help me to* resist *him.* But sitting in that dark, empty theater next to Aaron Stone, I had a sinking feeling that God could no longer reach me.

October 17, 2010
She's Mine; You Can't Have Her

The day I crossed the line was in early October. I allowed him to come into my house. My son was out of town and I was home alone. Aaron texted me and asked me to meet him for a drink. As usual, I answered without thinking: 'Why don't you come over here? It's a nice night and we can have a few drinks out on my deck.'

'Sounds great; I will be over in twenty minutes,' he texted back.

Alone time, yes! Now, I can question him about Kyle's research without the risk of someone else overhearing. Maybe I was trying to justify the fact that I was going against my own better judgment.

As soon as the doorbell rang, I peeked around the curtain and out the window. Aaron stood on my doorstep, in a black leather jacket, with his usual confident posture. Adrenaline surged through my body as I opened the door.

"Hi Aaron, come on in."

"Thank you, Angela. You look breathtaking, as always." I felt myself blush, suddenly feeling self-conscious about Aaron seeing my house. I analyzed my furniture and the art on my walls as we walked through the living room and into my kitchen.

"Can I pour you a glass of wine, Aaron?"

"Of course," he replied, smiling as he glanced around.

While I was pouring his wine, I watched him out of the corner of my eye. He'd noticed the guitar in the corner of the living room and stooped to pick it up.

"I never could play a damn thing on that guitar," I admitted, making small talk.

"I taught myself how to play," Aaron replied. "Let me bring it out onto the deck and I'll play for you."

"That's fine, as long as you play it better than I do," I answered with a teasing smile. After a few drinks, we sat chatting on the deck. He began to play the chords of a familiar song and my thoughts wandered to Kyle. I wasn't ready to deal with that…

"Hey," I said, interrupting him, "I want to go inside and watch a movie. How does that sound?"

"Fine, as long as you let me hold you," Aaron replied with a slick smile. Once we'd agreed on a movie, Aaron went straight for the long brown chaise and laid down on it. He motioned for me to come lay down next to him and I, somewhat reluctantly, complied.

He put his arms around me, whispering over and over, "Angela, my Angela. You're my Angela."

The words put me in a strange hypnotic kind of trance, but I didn't fight it because it felt good just to be held again. I'd almost forgotten what an incredible sensation affection could be.

When he stopped whispering, I looked up at him, but his eyes did not meet mine. He was staring steadily at the wall, but his eyes were empty, as though he saw nothing there. I looked up at him, he was looking towards the wall steadily; but he wasn't really looking at the wall. Abruptly, he began shouting at the wall as though someone else was in the room with us. "She's mine! *You* can't have her! She's *mine*! Angela is *mine*!"

I immediately stood up, looking back and forth between Aaron and the spot on the wall to which his eyes were glued. *Who the hell does he see? Who is he talking to?* I blinked, but I couldn't see anyone. *Why does he keep insisting that I'm his? He's acting like I'm his property!* Without a word, I backed down the hall, not taking my eyes off of him, until I had reached the bathroom. I needed to feel safe. I locked the door behind myself and flipped on the light. One of the bulbs above the vanity popped as it burnt out and I jumped, letting out a small yelp. I looked in the mirror, taking deep breaths to calm myself down, and attempted to rationalize what I had seen and heard.

Less than a minute passed when there was a small, but firm knock on the bathroom door. I took one last deep breath and opened the door. Aaron leaned against the doorframe. "Are you alright, Angela?" he asked, his soothing voice entirely different from the one he'd just used to shout at the wall. I nodded, but both of us knew it

37

was a non-verbal lie. Aaron pulled me close and began to kiss my neck. Our breathing grew intense and panic began to wash over me.

"Aaron." I pushed him back and his piercing eyes glared into mine. "Aaron, I'm not ready for this." His passionate countenance dissipated into anger.

"How long are you going to wait, Angela?" he demanded. "Your husband walked out on you. He's not coming back—he's with another woman."

His words shattered what fragile hope I had left inside. It wasn't as if his words weren't true; though harsh and cold, he spoke simply of my reality. No matter how much I wished and prayed, Kyle was never coming back.

That moment, in the hallway of my empty home, became a turning point in my life, and certainly not for the good. Memories flooded my mind; I remembered all of the nights I had laid in my bed alone, crying and begging God to bring my husband back. I had fasted for days, waking up every night at three o'clock in the morning to go into the bathroom to pray facedown on the floor, pleading with God for my husband to return home. I thought about all those wasted words and sleepless nights. I realized for the first time that what I had been holding onto so tightly had slipped through my grip like a handful of sand. My reply to Aaron took the last bit of strength I had. "If you care about me, then you will wait." And wait he did.

November 5, 2010
Break in the Family Tree

Aaron and I started to spend a lot of time together. I hadn't told my son, Nick, that we were something of an item, although he did ask when he saw us together. I simply told him that we were just friends. One afternoon, Aaron and I were lying on my couch watching TV when Nick and one of his friends walked in. I'll never forget the expression on Nick's face; it showed surprise mixed with anger. I wondered if he and Kyle had spoken. He must have been upset that the man who claimed to associate with Lucifer had his arms wrapped around his beloved mother. "Ma, can I talk to you alone for a minute?" Nick's face was flushing redder by the second.

"Sure." I untangled myself from Aaron's arms and winked down at him. Once we were alone in the garage, I folded my arms across my chest, ready for the confrontation I knew was coming. "What's up, Nick?"

"What are you doing, Mom?" Nick blurted out. "I thought you two were just friends. Why the hell is he in our house? What is wrong with you? Dad told you what Aaron believes! He claims that he *is* Lucifer. Come on, Mom. Get him *out* of our house!" Nick turned and walked out, slamming the garage door behind him. As the sound echoed against the metal door and the concrete floor, my heart sunk. I never wanted to upset or hurt Nick; he was the only one who had been by my side during those two long years. I felt mixed emotions overwhelm me. I loved my son with all of my heart, but I was falling for the one person he told me to stay away from. It was not my intention to start any drama; I felt I had to tell Aaron that it might be best to stay away for now—just until things with Nick cooled down. When I rejoined Aaron on the sofa and shared my concerns, he snapped at me. "Who is the mother here and who is the child?" I felt like the rope in tug-of-war. I was being pulled back and forth between the emotions I felt for the two of them. Although I felt torn, the hold Aaron had on me was too strong to fight against. *He's blinding me with his affection,* I realized. *He set the trap, I fell for it, and now my ability to think rationally is gone. Even my son can't reach me here. Open your eyes, Angela! Aaron is deceiving you!*

I had to comply with Nick's wishes because they were in my best interest. "Aaron, I think you should leave." Those piercing eyes seared into mine. "What did you say?" he demanded.

"I think you should leave," I repeated. He took a step toward me and I flinched. Something in his expression changed. He turned his back on me, grabbed his jacket, and slammed my front door behind him. Taking a deep breath and shutting my eyes as tightly as I could, I silently thanked God that Aaron Stone had not laid a hand on me.

November 21, 2010
Pulling the Gun

When Aaron could no longer come to my house, he spent more time with Bob, which made it easier for me to see him after work. I could tell he wasn't thrilled with the decision I had made, but he seemed to respect what I felt was right. One night, while we were sitting alone on Bob's back deck, Aaron pulled me onto his lap and told me to look into his eyes. My gut instinct told me not to, but he was persistent. I pushed myself away from him and stood up. "I'm cold," I said. "Let's go back inside."

Although he had me under his spell, I knew better than to look directly into Aaron's eyes. As I turned my back to go inside, I could have sworn I heard him let out a low growl. I slid Bob's patio door closed behind me and grabbed my purse from the kitchen counter. "Thanks for having me over, Bob," I said as I headed for the front door.

"You're leaving?" he asked, surprised. He was just putting the finishing touches on the mint juleps he'd been preparing.

"Yes, I forgot…I have to be up early in the morning," I lied.

41

"Okay…" I left Bob there in the kitchen, Aaron on the deck, and hurried home.

That night, and several nights that followed, I had intense nightmares. I found myself fighting demons that were after me. Although He felt far away during my waking hours, when I was asleep, God always seemed to speak His words to me. A still, small voice would whisper phrases from the Scripture and I suddenly knew how to fight the evil spirits in my nightmares. I remember one most vividly. I was in the labyrinth in the dark of night, begging God to show me what I needed to do. Suddenly, I felt a strong force wrap itself around my legs, trying to take me. "No weapon formed against me shall prosper," I heard myself say. The demon immediately let me go. The scene before me changed.

I was binding spirits together and they launched themselves into the sky, taking me with them. Oddly, I was not afraid. I persisted. As I began to feel weak, God opened my eyes. He reminded me of what happens when I use the name of Jesus. The spirits turned black, like ash, and crumbled away.

After a few of these dreams, I felt compelled to begin keeping a journal of my nightmares. They were warning signs I should have heeded, driving me in the opposite direction of Aaron Stone. But any time the phone rang, I hoped it was him. My heart beat faster at the thought of racing to meet him.

* * * *

The three of us were hanging out at Bob's house one night when Bob was unusually quiet. We were all watching TV; Aaron and I were on the couch together. I always suspected that Bob was jealous of the affection Aaron and I showed to each other. But the same could be said of anyone who saw us together; everyone wanted what we had. "What's wrong, Bob? You've barely spoken," I finally pointed out.

"I didn't get much sleep last night. Nightmares," he mumbled.

"I'm sorry," I said sincerely, thinking of my own nightmares. "What happened in them?"

"I need a drink," Bob said, as though he hadn't even heard me. He pushed himself to his feet, found his keys, and was out the door within seconds. Aaron and I didn't let Bob's exit keep us from enjoying out time together—we kept watching TV. Once Aaron had fallen asleep, I kissed him on the forehead and left for home.

I woke up at 5am to my phone blaring in my ear. I'd fallen asleep with it on my pillow. I was surprised it still had a charge since I had forgotten to plug it in. I caught the call just before it went to voicemail, answering blearily. "Hello?"

"Angela!" Aaron's voice came across sharply on the line. "You have to come over to Bob's right now!"

"Why, what's wrong? What happened?"

"It's Bob! He pulled a gun on me an hour ago. I called the police. They are taking him to some sort of mental institution," Aaron's usually calm voice had an edge to it. Although I hadn't known Bob for very long, it took me several seconds to process the frightening information.

"Oh my goodness, are you okay?" My heart had begun to pound against my chest. *And to think, I left only a few short hours ago.*

"Please, Angela, come over quickly," he pleaded. Before I could respond, he'd hung up the phone. I jumped out of bed, threw on some sweats, and ran out the door. I raced over to Bob's house and saw the ambulance pulling away with Bob safely inside. When I opened his front door, I saw a glittering mess of glass everywhere...*probably the remnants of a very recent fight.*

As I sidestepped the broken statues, I spied Aaron, seated on one of the kitchen chairs. His expression was one of shock and anger.

"Oh my God, Aaron, what happened? When I left you were asleep on the couch."

"Yes, I was. But Bob came home and started yelling at me about being the Antichrist. He was slapping the tattoos on my hands. He picked up the glass statues from his shelf and hurled them angrily across the room. I told him to sit down, chill out, and explain to me what was wrong. He came up with this elaborate story, claiming that he was a hit man paid to kill me," Aaron continued with a fierce look. "He walked into the bedroom, and the next thing I knew, he emerged with a gun pointed at my head. He said he was going to kill the Antichrist. I jumped up and grabbed the gun where it was cocked. I pushed Bob down on the floor and scrambled to unload the gun. I tried to question him…about who was trying to kill me, but he was no help. He just kept going on and on about how they were going to kill him because he didn't complete the job. He was so out of it; he really wouldn't give me any answers. He told me he was going to shoot himself if I left him alone. I told him I was going to call you, but I actually called the police. They came and took the gun, then loaded him onto an ambulance."

"Holy crap, that's crazy." A nagging thought crept into my mind. *What if there is more to the story than he is telling you? How do you know that he's telling you the truth?*

Due to Bob's required stay at the institution, I didn't get to speak to him for days. When he was finally out, I called him and asked him to meet me for coffee. He agreed. Once we sat down with our cappuccinos, I asked Bob to tell me what had really happened that night. "Angela, I've tried, but I don't remember a thing. Obviously something happened, but I can't seem to remember how it started…" His tone and expression turned from his cappuccino to me. "Are you still going to church, Angela?"

"Yes, of course. Why do you ask?" I heard defense in my voice.

"Well I'm sure that your association with Aaron will soon put a stop to that." *Why would Bob say that? This is all so strange.*

I realized that Bob probably hadn't known me long enough to understand my convictions. "Let me tell you something, Bob, I love my church and I love God and nothing is going to keep me from that. Not even Aaron, if he actually is the Antichrist. Lucifer himself couldn't change that; I can't alter my heart from loving Jesus. It's just something deep within my heart and soul—something I have felt for years."

"That's a good thing, Angela. Don't let go of that. Stay strong," Bob said with a smile. "I've got to go, work calls." With that, Bob gave me a hug and a quick peck on the cheek. He whispered in my ear, "Be careful," and walked out the door.

As I sipped my cappuccino, thoughts swirled about in my mind. *Wow, all of this is getting pretty deep. What did I get myself into? It's time to do some of my own research on Aaron Stone.*

When I got home, I booted up my computer and started digging deeply into everything that had ever been published about Aaron. Not only had he publicly referred to himself as "Lucifer incarnate" and "the Antichrist," but other people had made mention of the fact that he had appeared out of *nowhere*. There were no school records before high school, no family history, *nothing*.

Oh my God! I thought to myself. *They're saying these things about my boyfriend! What if this stuff is true? He is so charming and loveable...how can he be Lucifer?* I sat back and thought about everything I had witnessed while I was with him. The way his voice changed when he was on business calls, the mysterious glowing eyes, the sinister laughter...

For the first time, I realized that there were two sides to Aaron Stone. And I was in love with one of them.

* * * *

Aaron's affection was something I never had to question; he loved me and I knew that. My phone rang. I looked down and realized it was Aaron calling.

"Angela."

"Hey, Aaron, I was just thinking about you."

"Aw, I'm always thinking about you, my love. Listen, I want you to get ready. I am on my way to pick you up; the two of us are going to have a nice, quiet dinner tonight."

I loved his spontaneity. I answered back quickly, "How much time do I have before you arrive?"

"I'll be there in thirty minutes, Angela. Wear something comfortable. I want to dance tonight." I felt the flutters in my stomach even when he spoke to me over the phone.

"Great! See you in thirty, love." *Thirty minutes! How am I supposed to be dressed, ready, and perfect for Aaron in thirty minutes?* I ran toward my closet and looked for the sexiest, most comfortable dress I owned. My gaze landed on a form-fitting red dress. I slid it off of its hanger, draped it over my arm, grabbed a pair of matching red stilettos, and headed for the shower.

Before I knew it, I heard a knock on the door. I was fastening the clasp of a diamond necklace Aaron had given me a few days earlier, but I stopped to run for the door. As soon as I opened it, Aaron's piercing green eyes and his charismatic smile made me feel like a schoolgirl going out on her first date.

Aaron walked in, put down his phone, and turned around to face me. "Angela, you look absolutely stunning tonight. Red is the perfect color for you." He put his arms around me and bent to kiss me gently on the cheek. He whispered in my ear, "Tonight will be an evening you will never forget. I'm going to treat you like a princess."

Heading downtown, Aaron's limousine stopped in front of a small, but elegant, Italian restaurant. I smiled to myself, knowing that he'd picked a restaurant that served my favorite, authentic Italian, because he knew how difficult it is to come by in Nashville. This thoughtful gesture was very commonplace—his actions always showed his sensitive side and he frequently went out of his way to please me.

"Before we go in, Angela, there is something I want to give you." Aaron reached into his pocket and pulled out a small, square gift box wrapped in crisp, red paper. It had a black, satin bow on top.

"Oh, Aaron. I don't know what to say. You spoil me!"

He smiled and said, "You deserve to be spoiled, my love. And how perfect it is that you wore red—the same color I chose to wrap your gift." As I tore open the red paper, I felt my heart racing in anticipation. *What can it be?* I lifted the lid of the gift box and the light gleamed against the sparkling red ruby earrings. *How perfect!* I'd forgotten to add earrings to my ensemble when I heard him knock on the door.

"Put them on, Angela," Aaron coaxed. "They were made to perfectly match your gorgeous dress." *How had Aaron known that I would wear my red dress?*

I looked into his eyes as I felt tears welling up in my own. "How did you know that I would be wearing a red dress tonight, Aaron?"

He laughed. "I just have a sixth sense about what pleases you, Angela."

I put my arms around him, kissed him on the cheek, and whispered, "This is the side of you that I love—the Aaron that I could spend the rest of my life with."

Aaron grinned. "Come on, Angela, our reservation is in five minutes and we can't be late." Before I could even get my seatbelt off, he had climbed out and was at the door on my side of the limo, holding the door open for me. As I accepted his extended hand, he said, "Watch your step, Mademoiselle." I couldn't help but notice that his whit, button-down dress shirt and his black, Armani suit jacket made him look extremely debonair.

As we headed into the restaurant, the hostess at the front greeted us. "Welcome to Giovani's. Do you have a reservation?"

Aaron smoothly replied, "Stone, Aaron Stone. Table for two." Aaron towered over the short, stout hostess as she searched the computer for our reservation. Her big, brown eyes glanced at us as she acknowledged the reservation. "Ah, yes, here you are. Table for two. Follow me, please."

As we made our way through the crowd toward our table, I could hear soft music drifting from an upstairs piano. Off in the corner sat a quaint little table for two. Two red roses sat on the tabletop among three votive candles. The candles cast an illuminating glow over the roses.

As Aaron helped me slip my jacket off, I felt his warm hands skim over my shoulders and down my arms. He leaned over and kissed the back of my shoulder, whispering into my ear, "May I remind you again of how special you are? And there is no other place I would rather be than here with you tonight, Angela."

I slid into my seat and leaned over to take in the aroma of the roses. Aaron gazed into my eyes and said, "I bought two roses—one represents the love we share now, and the second is for the future we will soon share."

It was a lovely night. The romance in the air was almost palpable. I never wanted the evening to end. The sadness I'd felt when my husband left seemed to melt away. Aaron treated me like a queen and the way he made me feel was overwhelming. It was a feeling I wanted to last forever.

January 15, 2011
My Exorcism of Deliverance

In December, I moved out of my house and into a town home about ten miles away. Now that he had the ability to come and go as he pleased, Aaron was thrilled. Nick had decided not to move with me. He said it was time for him to move on with his life, but deep down, I knew it was because of Aaron.

My relationship with Aaron had put a strain on my relationship with Nick. There was a gap in the closeness we'd once shared. I couldn't blame my son for struggling with my decision to date a man who claimed to be Lucifer, but I also couldn't seem to help myself. It wasn't just Nick who appeared to disappear. My girlfriends seemed to distance themselves as well. My phone calls started to go unreturned. *I wonder why this keeps happening—maybe they are just scared to be around me? Or is it something more; is Aaron casting some sort of spell to push everyone out of my life?*

I thought about the way Aaron disappeared every time there was a full moon. He always seemed to have an excuse as to why, but I was too afraid of the truth to press for answers. Fear was a constant companion. I knew I needed deliverance. I secretly did some research online and found a man who claimed to perform exorcisms. He was holding a conference in Nashville in January, so I called to schedule a private appointment with him. Weeks passed and I almost didn't have the nerve to go see the man. As I was walking into the building to meet with him, I received a text from Aaron.

'Where are you, Angela?'

I was afraid to text him back, as if he would know from my response where I was and what I was about to do.

'Why aren't you answering me, Angela?'

Anxiety nearly paralyzed me, but something inside of me was determined to keep the appointment. *I can do this*, I told myself. When I walked into the lobby, a short man with thinning hair in a brown suit approached me. A woman with long, blonde hair and soft blue eyes was right behind him. The man extended his hand for me to shake.

"Hello, Angela," he said in a welcoming tone. "I'm Mike and this is my assistant, Karen. I'm so happy you made it. Are you ready to begin?"

"As ready as I can be," I replied with a wavering smile.

They walked me into a room that had a soft armchair in the center of the room and motioned for me to sit. Mike took the seat across from me while Karen remained standing ready to take notes.

"Sit down, please, and do make yourself comfortable," said Mike. I noticed a cross and a Bible sitting on an end table next to his chair. *It's not really me who should be having this deliverance— Aaron Stone is the one who needs it!* I thought to myself.

Mike asked me several questions and when I began to talk about Aaron, his questions became very direct. From the questions he asked, I knew that he had read about Aaron and the strange claims he made.

"You must be very important in God's Kingdom," Mike said gently.

"Why would you say that?"

"Because the Devil didn't send one of his demons to derail you—he came himself. If he has you next to him, he doesn't have to worry about you, Angela. Thus, God must have a very important mission for you to warrant this kind of attention form Lucifer. Do you know what God's mission is?"

"No, I am not sure what I am supposed to do."

"Remember, God loves you and the Bible says, 'No weapon formed against you will prosper.'" Those words struck a chord within me. They were the words I'd said in my nightmare. *But where did I hear them recently?* A memory flashed back from a few months earlier. I was getting my nails done when my mentor, Rachel, called me.

"Angela, I want to give you a Scripture." It was the very same one Mike had quoted. *What is God trying to tell me through all of this?*

Mike told me to get rid of everything that belonged to Aaron. He told me not to answer his phone calls or texts, and to certainly not allow him into my home.

When I left the appointment, I was scared out of my mind, but I did what Mike told me to do. When I got home, I packed up all of Aaron's belongings and dropped them off at his business partner's house. Afraid to ignore his calls, let alone receive them, I turned my phone off. I also changed the locks on my doors because I knew he had a key.

At first, I really tried to stay away from him. This Aaron prohibition only lasted about a month, though. I couldn't stop thinking about him—almost as if he had the ability to draw me back to him. The feeling grew stronger and more intense by the day. I had never been much of a drinker, so I couldn't even use alcohol as an escape from the pain and loneliness that tormented me. I started going out with my girlfriends every night just so I wouldn't be home alone. After one such girls' night, when I felt particularly alone, I just wanted to text Aaron to say hi. I finally worked up the courage to send the text around 2:30am, but I never heard back from him that night. *What was I thinking, why am I opening the door to him again?* The very next day I received a text from him. 'I was sleeping when you texted me, but hi.'

'How are you doing?'

'I'm doing well. You must have been out late last night, huh buddy?' We exchanged a few more texts, and then came the question.

'What are you doing for lunch?'

Don't do it, Angela, was my initial reaction, but then again, I had already opened the door. 'I am getting my hair done at 11:15.'

'Well, what time do you want to meet?'

'Where are you?'

'In town. Meet me at the mall.' I picked him up at the mall and we went to the steakhouse across the street for lunch. One of the booths near the bar was open, so we sat ourselves. His eyes seemed to stare straight through me. I noticed his eyes began to shine with tears. "Why did you do that to me, Angela? Why did you leave me?" *I can't tell him. He can't know that I'm afraid of him.*

"I'm sorry…After my divorce, I feel so confused about what I want in my life at this point, Aaron." I was also afraid that he would find out about the man named Mike who had performed an exorcism on me. *What would he think of me going there? What would he do to me if he found out I went there?* We chatted a little more as I pushed my thoughts aside.

"Will I see you after work tonight, Angela?"

"Text me later and we'll see." Sure enough, right as nine o'clock rolled around, I got the text.

'Will I be seeing you tonight, Angela?'

'I'm not sure, Aaron.'

'Why not? Just come and get me, please. I have been drinking and I don't want to drive.' Part of me wanted to see him so badly. But another part of me was warning me not to go.

'Are you coming, Angela? I'm waiting for you?'

'Okay, okay, I am on my way.'

When I arrived at Billy's house, Aaron was so happy to see me. He had never looked so good as he did sauntering over to my car. Once he climbed in, he leaned over and gave me a long kiss. It felt like a bolt of electricity ran through my body.

When we arrived at my place, I felt guilty. I knew in my heart that I was making a big mistake by letting him into my home and into my life again, but I felt such overwhelming affection for him that it was so difficult to say no. So I said yes instead. I walked straight into the kitchen with Aaron on my heels.

He swept me into his arms and said, "Promise me, Angela, promise me you will never do that again. I love you—don't ever leave me again."

He cradled my face in his warm hands and kissed me forcefully. *How could I ever have left him?* "I promise, Aaron, I will never do that to you again." *Did I just seal my own death sentence with a kiss?*

February 19, 2011
Possessed or Psychopath?

I made the mistake of looking into his eyes one night while we were watching a movie at my house. "What do you see, Angela?" he asked. I looked away, but he tilted my head so I was looking back into his eyes. "What do you see?" he persisted.

At first I couldn't see anything, which seemed to anger him. He told me I wasn't focused enough. So I kept looking and I finally saw what he wanted me to see—the whites of his eyes began to turn red and his pupils elongated. I jerked my head back in disbelief. *I can't believe what I am seeing!*

"What did you see, Angela?"

"Well, I'm not exactly sure, but whatever that was…Aaron, it was weird." I didn't want to look anymore. I was done playing his games. *Just ask him to tell you what you saw. He wants to tell you anyway and his answer can't be any worse than the explanations you're imagining…*

"What was that, Aaron?"

"It's *him*. He is the one who handles all of the phone calls and the business affairs. He is the strong one within me. But there is also someone else."

"Someone else?" I asked, trying to remain calm.

"A female." As though suddenly taking on the attributes of a female, Aaron's hand caressed my cheek. In a soft, higher-pitched voice, he told me that I was a good, loving person; he told me that I was very special. After hearing that woman and even that man speaking through him, when Aaron would come back, his voice was like a small child in comparison. *Oh. My. God. Am I dealing with demon possessing or Schizophrenia here?* Oddly, I didn't feel threatened by Aaron's other personalities each time he shared them with me. I didn't care for the tone or mannerisms of the powerful businessman inside of him. He was the jerk of the three—very aggressive, self-centered, and quick to anger if things didn't go his way. I suddenly understood where Aaron's anger came from.

"Aaron," I would whisper gently. "Come back."

Aaron was sweet and loving. All he needed was love in return. I know that all of this must sound insane, but I began to believe that I was supposed to take care of Aaron. I had to protect him from the other personalities. I had to pray for him and stop the other two from overpowering him.

The aggressive one told me that he was the one chosen to bring about the New World Order. He would tell me that I would believe it when I saw it happen in 2012. I found myself searching the Internet for new information. The same questions rang out in my mind over and over again. *Is he really the Antichrist, Lucifer? Or could he possibly be an alien? He could just be possessed. Well, I guess all of these theories are a little strange, otherworldly even. What normal explanations could there possibly be for this man?* I needed answers and I needed them soon. The things he promised were coming were just around the corner. *I need to be prepared, just in case.*

Through those many Internet searches I would find articles that caused me to recollect conversations that Aaron and I had together, as well as how Aaron was never afraid to admit freely that he worshipped Satan. He always felt that the church was the evil one, lying to people and controlling them with fear. I loved my church. I knew the only fear I felt came from Aaron, but I wasn't strong enough to fight it.

I read that people under Lucifer's power work spells on the people around them. I thought of some of the strange things that had happened to me when I was away from Aaron. Even though his control over me was taxing, physically and mentally, I still felt maddeningly attracted to him. I couldn't walk away. He would hold me in his arms and my heart would simply melt. I guess I had finally come to terms with my situation—I had fallen in love with the Antichrist. *Does this mean that I am damned to hell? But what I struggle with the most, though, is that I love God. No matter how far away He feels, I acknowledge Him as my Master and Creator. Jesus is my Savior...but I feel as though Aaron is trying to separate us. So, what do I do?* Trying to reconcile my warring ideals, I realized that

Aaron needed to know God's love. No matter what he said or did, I would love him with Christ's love. I wanted to show him what real love looked like.

February 23, 2011
Holding to His Story

Anytime I asked Aaron about his family, I got the same vague story. There were no details about how he grew up or about his father. He would only tell me fragments of a story that seemed completely impossible. His mother had conceived him on an airbase and given birth to him in the middle of winter on December twenty-first. "I know nothing about my father. All I know is that I'm half human and half alien," Aaron stated, matter-of-factly. His stories were always unbelievable, but this one especially. But I reminded myself that there was still a possibility that he could be possessed. And I *had* promised to love him, no matter what.

Remember the way his eyes turned red that night? A part of me recalled how scared I'd been. *Remember first meeting those other personalities? Most women would probably have gotten the hell out of this relationship if they experienced half of the oddities that I have. But not me. How and why did I fall in love with a psychopath?* Aaron was not in any way abusive to me. He displayed his love for me in such a unique and strange way. It wasn't even sexual. *I am not held by abuse—I am not held by sex. So what is it? Is it loneliness?*

Somewhere inside of me, I knew the answer. The family that I had once cherished had fallen apart. I was trying to fill my own void. But I should have known how much it would cost me in the end.

March 2, 2011
Keeping My Eyes Open

After months of watching Aaron closely and really seeing him with my own eyes, I found myself listening to his phone calls. They were coming in from all over the world. Or were they?

If what he had told me was the truth and he was part alien, was it possible that the calls were coming from other worlds? *Back to the Internet.* I pulled up pictures of aliens just to see if I could make out any resemblance. Aaron's body features were certainly different from any man I had ever been with. His fingers were shaped differently than the average human's fingers. The ones in the photos looked very similar. Even the hair on his arms and legs was not normal. His hair had a strange V shape to it, but the bottom of his legs were bare. I'd asked him about it once.

"Aaron, do you shave the bottom of your legs?"

"No! I'm different, Angela. I told you that," he replied in a somewhat exasperated manner.

"Is that why your fingers are shaped so oddly, too?" I shot back at him with a teasing grin.

"Maybe they look like my father's fingers," he laughed.

"Maybe," I tried to join his lightheartedness.

Something else stood out to me about Aaron. He had a photographic memory and the ability to recall details that the average human would probably miss. "Do you retain every single word of every single movie you see?" I asked one night after he quoted a line I had never paid attention to.

"My mind is incredibly advanced, Angela. If I told you some of the things I know it would frighten you."

He smiled and kissed my forehead, murmuring quietly, "You're special, Angela. You're very special." I never got tired of hearing that he loved me and how special I was, but at times it felt like a distraction.

"Seriously, how do you do it?"

"I told you before that I am not human—why will you not believe me?" *Maybe he is an alien that just happened to fall in love with a simple, human woman who can appreciate that love. Or maybe he is here to experience what humans deem to be love.* I tried my best to convince myself of anything that led me away from the idea that the man I loved so much was Lucifer incarnate.

Either way, I couldn't fight the deep connection I felt to him. We still had obstacles just as every relationship does. I hated it when he drank, but I was amazed by the sheer quantity of alcohol he consumed. It did nothing to him at all; he drank alcohol like a normal person would drink water. When I would confront him about it, he would say, "Angela, I am just a professional drinker," and then laugh it off. *Or are you an alien upon whose system alcohol has no effect?* And, of course, alcohol was not his only vice. I watched him smoke a whole cigar one night. As soon as he put it out, he leaned over to give me a kiss. I immediately pulled back thinking that his breath would be disgusting from the cigar. His breath took me aback though—there was no trace of the smelly cigar he had just smoked. *Come on, how can this be? Everyone knows how much cigars stink.* My eyes were open, but they were trying to ignore what had been there all along.

April 19, 2011

Who is Aaron Stone?

The bottom line of Aaron's claims was that he needed to create the One World Government, a benign dictatorship, in order to save the planet. He told me that there were a lot of different alien races occupying the Earth at the same time, each with different agendas, much like the governments of Earth. Aaron's hope was that a One World Government would unite them all in support of his goals. According to Aaron, among the most powerful alien races were the "Dracos" (the Reptoids) from Alpha Draco, and the Reptilians from the Orion constellation.

Earth's alien visitors, I was told, saw themselves as superior beings to us. They were displeased with the way Evolution had turned out. Aaron said that if he should fail to convince these alien races to follow his plan, they would destroy the Earth to kill off the human population.

"Humanity has failed," he said to me once, "I will create a better way, a new beginning." *Yes, humanity has 'failed.' But we deserve a second chance. We do not need to be put under the control of Aaron Stone's emissaries on Earth. Whatever redemption Aaron is bringing to us, I can still hold onto hope that it will turn things around.*

From everything Aaron had told me, his goal was to create a better society for mankind. He was in favor of a benevolent dictatorship that would end what he called 'the cancer of society,' Congress. He told me that when people are educated about his plan, they would voluntarily choose it. "The answer lies in the Urantia Book. I stand with the seven Prince Power Directors and the Ancient of Days," he explained, but I didn't truly understand what any of that meant.

Apparently, it was up to them to determine when Aaron would receive his full power. It was he who fell from grace and now it is he who might be redeemed. That is his reasoning for being in favor of humanity's redemption. "Look at it this way, Angela," he said, "I am on all sides—I am beyond good and evil. I am in the Urantia Book, the Celestial Bible. It is so important that every United States President has a copy of it in the Oval Office—the Blue Book."

Who is this man I am dating? I wondered. *This guy books flights to New York City or Washington DC at the last minute and just leaves me for days on end. I'm lucky if I receive one text a day from him while he's gone. Everything he does is so hush-hush; he never goes into details about his work. Yet I stick around, waiting for him to return. My friends would say I'm a fool for putting up with this.* Thought swam in my head, but I didn't ask questions.

Before one such secret trip, Aaron told me he would be back in three days. Yet there I was, two weeks later, and he had still not returned home. I finally sent him a text: 'Hey Aaron, if you would like to end our relationship I would understand and be totally fine with that. Just give me your blessing and I will move on.'

The next day, he answered: 'Angela, you know I love you. I will come home today just to prove it to you. Want to pick me up at the airport?'

And of course, I was over the moon to hear from him. I texted back excitedly: 'What time and what airline? I will be there.'

When that plane arrived, he didn't need to worry—I was there waiting for him. I began to feel like I was *always* waiting for him.

September 9, 2011
The Chip

After a few months of Aaron's sporadic traveling, I began to get used to it. I would spend time with my friends to distract myself from the fact that he was gone so often. I made plans one night with my girlfriend, Denver. She suggested that we go to a local restaurant for a glass of wine. While enjoying our wine and some long overdue girl talk, I suddenly felt an excruciating pain racing down my spine. It was as if an electric pulse was shocking me. "Denver, I feel a strange sensation going down my spine, as odd as that sounds... I'm going to the restroom. I'll be right back."

"Are you okay, Angela?"

"I'm not sure...I feel really lightheaded. It's almost like there's something in my neck that's burning." I stood up and hurried down a long hallway, looking for the bathrooms. Walking woozily along, I came upon a bench outside the bathroom and had to sit down for a minute. Opening my Louis Vuitton purse, I grabbed my cell phone from its depths. As I looked down to see what time it was, I abruptly felt the vibrations from the phone's energy shoot up the back of my neck. I quickly shut off my phone and ran into the bathroom. *Something is NOT right.*

I splashed cold water onto my face. *What the hell just happened?* As panicked as I was, I tried to regain my composure. *Calm down, Angela, don't freak yourself out.* I took a deep breath, checked my hair in the mirror, and returned to the table where Denver was waiting for me with a concerned look on her face. I couldn't speak. I just stared at Denver, but she must have read the fear I couldn't keep out of my eyes.

"Angela, are you okay?"

"I'm not sure." My voice came out barely above a whisper. "Denver, I know I can tell you anything, right?"

"Of course!"

"Have you ever heard of microchips?" I asked.

"Yes, but…Angela, why are you asking me that? You're freaking me out!" Denver said, her eyes searching for eavesdroppers before locking onto mine. My mind drifted away from our conversation. *Denver and I have been friends for a long time now; I can trust her.* Denver and I had initially bonded over early morning racquetball games. I considered her a close friend, but I still was uncertain if I could trust her with the things I knew about Aaron. *Surely she's known me long enough by now…*

When my ex-husband and I divorced, he told me it was time to sell our house. I immediately called my good friend Kaitlin, who lived two houses down from us, and asked her if she knew of a good real estate agent to help me sell the house.

"Yes, Angela, I know the perfect agent," Kaitlin reassured me. "Let's run up to Starbrew for a cup of coffee and I will find her number."

"Sure, Kaitlin."

"I'll pick you up in five minutes."

Kaitlin, who had just gone through a divorce herself, was a great friend. A few years prior, she had been diagnosed with multiple sclerosis and was struggling with the effects that it had on her body. She always told me it was God's way of telling her to slow down, to get out of the fast lane. For many years, Kaitlin had worked for a big automotive company, but after her diagnosis, she began to make drastic changes. Her husband, unwilling to bear the burden of the disease with her, asked for a divorce. Kaitlin's situation made me really wonder: *Why do bad things happen to good people?*

The friendship Kaitlin and I shared had become very important to me. Kaitlin attended a huge Baptist church, about five minutes away from our neighborhood. Even though I wasn't a Baptist, I accepted an invitation to visit with her. Surprisingly, I found that it was more like a nondenominational church than any Baptist church I had ever been to. The preacher was very down-to-earth and I started to look forward to attending every Tuesday night and Sunday morning. The spiritual journey I had taken a detour from began to flourish and a few months later, I made the decision to become a member.

Fellowship with believers seemed to soothe some of the pain Kaitlin and I felt after our divorces. We each had a choice. We could numb ourselves with pills and liquor, or fill the void with God. We chose God.

As we sat sipping our lattes at a cozy little corner table at Starbrew, Kaitlin reached into her pocket and pulled out the number of the recommended real estate agent.

"She's very well-known around here, Angela. When you're ready, you should definitely give her a call."

"I will, as soon as I get home," I promised. I was ready to get the whole thing over with. And because I knew I could trust Kaitlin's judgment, I trusted the woman whose name was on the card she'd given me. *Denver.* We finished our small talk and lattes and headed back home. As soon as I got into my house, I made the call and booked an appointment with Denver.

I will never forget the day I met Denver. When she arrived, a tall, blonde woman, with a slender figure and a walk that brimmed with confidence, I immediately felt at ease. I answered the door, taking in her soft, grayish blue eyes and bright smile that hinted at her bubbly personality. I think that was the moment I knew we were going to be great friends.

"ANGELA! Hello, stop spacing out! What were you saying about microchips?" *Oops, back to reality. What* was *I saying about microchips?* Denver seemed more than a little bit annoyed.

"Right…" I finally continued, in a hushed tone, "One night I couldn't sleep so Aaron told me to take a sleeping pill. The last thing I remember after taking it was Aaron standing over me, whispering in my ear, 'It won't hurt.' The next day, the back of my neck was extremely sensitive and itchy. And I know this sounds crazy, but I've noticed that every time I am around something electronic, I feel an eerie sensation running up my neck. It's like an electric pulse." I studied the expression on her face closely before I continued. "I'm not imagining things, Denver. I really think Aaron microchipped me." There was no denying it; Denver was completely confused. I had told her that he was eccentric, but she didn't know *everything*.

"Angela, why would he do that?" I looked away, shaking my head.

"I don't know for sure, but I think he wants to keep track of me. If he did put a chip in me, he knows my every move…" It was obvious that Denver wanted to comfort me, but she had no idea how. I realized that I needed to share it all with her. As she sat back against her seat, taking it all in, I told Denver everything I knew about Aaron.

"He loves you, Angela," she said, matter-of-factly, after I had finished. "Even if he *is* the Antichrist, I can't see him ever trying to hurt you. I don't understand how you've found a place in his heart, but you have. Regardless of Aaron's plans, we can't forget that God is still on the throne. He is very much in control of the paths that all of our lives are taking—including yours, Angela. Trust God and don't give up on your faith now! If you *are* in fact microchipped, God knows and has allowed it to happen. It's a part of His plan for you."

Denver's eyes gleamed brightly. I felt as though she could see into my soul. God was speaking through her and that reassured me in the midst of the confusion that overwhelmed me.

December 23, 2011
Under the Radar

Another trip to New York City came and went for Aaron. He stayed at my place for a few weeks and I tried to pretend that we were just playing the part of a totally average couple. It was hard to believe that this man, the one who occasionally wore off-brand blue jeans and usually drove a Nissan, could be the Antichrist. But I knew what I had seen. I knew what he had told me. And I finally believed all of it.

When pastors had spoken about the Antichrist, I'd pictured someone powerful, a man of great wealth, ruling the world and living a life of luxury. What I saw in Aaron was indeed a powerful man, but one who moved under the radar instead of in the public eye. He knew exactly what he was doing. Aaron was waiting quietly for the appointed moment when he would be commissioned to come onto the scene as the voice that would speak for the world. Although he had made it clear where his alliances where, Aaron was counting on the fact that the world would never even see him coming. They would be looking for a suave man to rise up and lead them. It was as if they were watching the front door while Aaron snuck in the back.

Aaron acted casual, but there were certainly moments where he craved luxurious indulgences. One night, he called me and said, "I feel like partying tonight, don't you? Let's go downtown—I'm thinking an ounce of cocaine should start our night off right." Cocaine was something that Aaron took great pleasure in.

"Come on, you know I hate that stuff."

"Angela, live for today. The pleasures this world has to offer are few and they will not be around forever…" His insistence was devilish.

"No, thank you," I grumbled, unwilling to go through that argument for the thousandth time. "I'll pass up one of the few so-called pleasures."

"You will never understand, will you? It's okay to indulge yourself, Angela. You have a free will and the ability to enjoy the present," Aaron sighed on the other end, frustrated. "But if you choose not to participate, I will not force that on you."

For months, I had watched him abuse his body with drugs and alcohol. I felt sad for the little boy inside of him. The evil entities that controlled him incessantly used him to fulfill their own pleasures without a thought for the loss of his innocence.

My own world was bursting with the evil influence of the spirit world. On an almost daily basis, Aaron had a way of making me see the real light of God through the darkness of his life. My struggle was not with Aaron, not with flesh and blood, but against the rulers, against the powers, against the forces of darkness, against the wickedness in heavenly places—in a nutshell, against everything that Aaron claimed to stand for.

I knew I was running out of time. In a few short days, it would be 2012. And, as Aaron promised, it would be the year he'd rise up. I just wasn't sure how to stop the ones inside of him without sabotaging the man I loved.

January 1, 2012
New Year's Eve

I heard the sound of a key turning in my door. I looked up and saw Aaron walk in, looking dapper in a black Hugo Boss suit.

"Wow, Aaron, you look great!"

"Of course, I am ringing in *my* year, Angela. Everything is ready to fall into place." I wasn't sure how to respond. I still had mixed emotions about what that could mean.

"What's ready to fall into place?"

"Like I've said before, just wait and see. My plan will come to fruition." His chuckle teetered on sinister. "Look at me, Angela." I obeyed. "The Aaron that is before you now will soon be replaced by one with far more power. They don't even know what they're looking for, but I will emerge from the shadows with the answers to their most desperate questions."

Folding himself into the space next to me on the sofa and crossing one leg over the other, he grinned. It was a grin that radiated euphoria.

"Can I get you something to drink?" I asked, suddenly needing to occupy myself with something other than my thoughts.

"I'd love a Jack and Coke. Thank you, love," he turned his gaze toward the television. *Where do I fit into this plan of his?* I wondered as I poured our drinks. *Why me?* As I rejoined him on the couch, his cell phone rang.

"Excuse me, Angela. I have to take this call; it's long distance from Croatia."

"Okay," I said, still holding our glasses, but he was already headed out onto my patio.

"*Zdravo*," I heard him say as the patio door slid shut. I glanced at the clock on my living room mantel. It was only six in the evening, but still, I wondered, *who does business on New Year's Eve?*

A few minutes passed and I heard the patio door slide open. Aaron reentered the room. "Everything okay?" I asked with a reassuring smile, handing him his drink.

"Absolutely perfect," he returned my smile as he accepted the drink and settled back beside me on the sofa. He swirled the ice around in his glass and took a long sip. "I have to fly to the Middle East for a few days, love," he said, turning his gaze toward me. "I have a meeting with a few members of the United Nations to discuss—" His phone rang again, cutting him off. "Sorry, I have to take this one, too," he apologized. This time, I detected him speaking German as he walked outside. *How many languages does this man know?*

It did seem like every other time I heard him speak on the phone it was in a different language. I walked into the kitchen, pretending I needed more ice for my cocktail, but I wanted to figure out what was going on. I could hear him going back and forth between English and German; I realized it was probably a conference call.

"There must be a diversion," I heard him say. "Details of this meeting must not leak out. It looks like 120 will be coming from our investors."

120? investors? Is he talking about money? I stood still with the door to the freezer slightly cracked open and continued to listen to his end of the conversation. "I've already spoken with most of Western Europe, the United States, and Canada. As we receive confirmation of their attendance, assure each of the ambassadors that we will be covering their flights." He seemed to be listening for a moment, so I began casually unloading the dishwasher. "I've already covered their meals and liquor. The caterers we've chosen have given me their word that we can change the head count until the day of. Just don't forget about the women."

I cringed. *The women? Oh, my God, what is this meeting about? Bribery? And more importantly, who is on the other end of Aaron's line? Who are his investors?*

"I just don't want any mistakes. You know how important it is that the currency is switched over within the fiscal year. We simply need them to provide the legislature and then we are free to make our move." *Is this how the New World Order starts? This invisible world government bribes its politicians to sell out their states and deceive their people? Isn't that treason? What a way to achieve their goal—through the world's finances, through money!* I could hear the conversation continue, but I wasn't really listening anymore. *Is this the kind of leader Aaron is going to become? All of the things he said about uniting the races and religions...was it just flowery words and good intentions?* I finally realized that it was time to get away from Aaron Stone.

The screen door slid open as Aaron came back inside from the patio. "What's wrong?" he asked, eyeing me carefully.

"Nothing..." I quickly came up with an excuse. "I was actually thinking, Aaron, that maybe after the New Year, I should set up a dinner date with Denver."

"That sounds fun. You haven't seen Denver in a while." *The microchip.* The one possibility that would ruin any chance of me getting away from Aaron Stone.

Aaron stood in front of my refrigerator, studying the pictures of my friends and family. He ran a finger over Denver's picture. "You've never mentioned my business to her, right? All of the conversations that I have, the ones you might overhear on occasion, are confidential and must not be repeated to anyone."

I felt as though his eyes were piercing straight through me. An instant that felt like an eternity later, he dropped his hand down to his side and his face softened. "But surely you *know* that already, love. I trust that you will not betray my trust, Angela." Though his words and his expression were gentle, the intensity behind them scared the hell out of me. I wondered if he knew what I'd said to Denver…I wondered if he knew what I was planning to *do* next.

January 21, 2012
Behind the Scene

Aaron was scheduled to leave for the Middle East in a few short weeks, which meant that I only had a short window of time to piece my escape plan together. When I made my call to Denver, I played it cool, knowing that my phone was probably tapped.

"Hey Denver, it's Angela. What are you doing Monday night?"

"Nothing that I know of. What's up, chica?"

"Are you up for dinner and a movie?"

"Yeah, that sounds great! Where would you like to meet?"

"Actually, would you mind picking me up? I'm thinking of dropping my car off for a tune-up."

"Sure Angela. Just be ready at five." I could almost hear my friend's smile over the phone and I smiled in return.

"Thanks, I will be!"

Aaron had been in the other room, but the second I hung up, he asked, "So, you're having dinner with Denver on Monday night?"

"Yes, Denver and I are going to grab something to eat and then head over to catch a movie."

"Well that sounds nice. You need to have some fun, Angela. You've looked stressed lately," Aaron remarked, searching my face curiously. My response was a smile, but my mind wondered, *Does it show that much?*

"Maybe you're right. There's been a lot going on at work lately. I guess I just didn't realize it was getting to me."

The next few days were torture. I tried to make sure I didn't do anything out of character. I didn't want to give Aaron any reason to suspect that my meeting with Denver was anything other than an innocent girls' night out.

Monday morning came and as I gave Aaron a quick kiss before leaving for work, I casually reminded him, "Hey baby, don't forget that I'm going out with Denver tonight."

"I haven't, love. Just remember what we talked about, Angela," he looked straight into my eyes as though he was warning me.

"I know, I know," I answered quickly, "I have to go or I'll be late for work."

"I'll be on calls all day, but I'll see you when you get done at work."

"Okay," I said. "Have a good day." He smiled and rolled back over. I grabbed my keys and headed out the door.

While I was at work, I struggled to concentrate. My mind raced with horrifying thoughts.

What happens if he finds out I am trying to leave him? I want to tell Denver about his business calls, but what would happen if he found out? I knew I had to snap out of it. My life was in God's hands.

At four thirty on the dot, I swiped my card to clock myself out and hurried out the door, glad that my workday was over. As I headed home, I thought about what it would be like to disappear. I wondered if anyone at work would ask where I'd gone. I imagined Aaron questioning the other employees on my whereabouts...I couldn't keep thinking about things like that.

Instead, I focused on the anticipation of finally being able to see Denver. I hurried up the three flights of stairs to my apartment, instructing myself to act *normal*, whatever that was anymore. Turning the key in the lock, I made sure I entered with a huge smile on my face. "Hey baby, I'm home!" I sung out, cheerily. "I'm going to hurry and jump in the shower so I can get ready for tonight."

Trying not to look at him, I walked quickly through the living room and into the bathroom, but Aaron was right behind me. He pulled me close and began kissing my neck.

"Let's make love before you go, Angela," he said a few moments later, caressing my shoulder. I turned to face him and saw that he was beginning to get undressed.

Why now? I thought with dismay. Our relationship had never been sexual; he made me feel more like a companion than his girlfriend at times. Honestly, I had given up on that aspect of our relationship due to the fact that the Book of Daniel talks about the

Antichrist not having a desire for women, which would make sense if he truly were the Antichrist. But now, when I was trying to get away from him, was not the time to express interest.

"Are you serious? Right now?"

"Why not, Angela?"

"Why not? Why now? We've gone several months together now without ever having sex and suddenly you want it? Seriously, you know that I have to leave soon. Denver is probably already on her way over here; I have to be ready to leave when she gets here."

"I just want to show you how much I *love* you, Angela."

"Can't you show me *later*, Aaron?"

"No, Angela, I want it now."

He pushed me into the bedroom, his hands still on my neck, and shoved me down on my bed. The strength behind his hands was so great I couldn't fight back. He choked me so I couldn't scream. As he began to force himself on me, I felt like I was watching it happen to me from somewhere else. Somewhere safe, somewhere sacred…anywhere else. That person on top of me was *not* the Aaron I knew. I looked into his eyes. They were bright red with the telltale, elongated pupils. The *other one* had overtaken Aaron. He brushed my hair back from my face and kept repeating, "You're all mine." Tears filled my eyes. I could barely breathe. My only thought was: *I have to get away from this monster.*

When he was finished, he released his grip on me and collapsed beside me. I put my feet on the floor, stood up, and reached for my robe. After wrapping it tightly around my shaking body, I tried to hold my sobs in my throat and I closed the bathroom door behind me. Letting the water warm up, I glanced at my reflection in the bathroom's unforgiving light. Scratches covered my breasts and thighs. I couldn't look anymore. I stepped into the shower, letting the hot water run over me, stinging my fresh wounds, and the sobs finally escaped. I scrubbed and scrubbed, but no amount of soap could make me feel clean.

Somehow I managed to pull myself together enough to finish showering and get dressed. Fighting tears, I was trying to finish my makeup when Denver texted me. 'I'm here.'

'Just touching up my makeup, I'll be down in a minute, I texted back.'

I walked out of the bathroom, afraid of the state I'd find Aaron in. He'd slipped into the living room while I was in the shower. As though nothing had happened, he sat quietly on the couch, flipping nonchalantly through the channels.

"Denver is here, Aaron, I've got to go now." He looked at me, traces of remorse in his gaze, but that look was gone in an instant, replaced by a confident smile.

"Okay, love," he said, pointing to his cheek.

Scared out of my mind, I bent to kiss the spot on his cheek he'd pointed to. "Angela," he said, leaning back to look up at me again. "You *do* understand that I didn't want to do that to you? I love you and would never hurt you. That wasn't *me*." Afraid to say anything, I just nodded and walked out the door so he wouldn't see my tears.

January 21, 2012 (continued)
Help Is On the Way

I practically ran down the three flights of stairs and jumped into Denver's car. "Hey, Angela," Denver's voice was cheerful, but I could feel her countenance change as she realized I was crying.

I was silent for a full five minutes, just staring out the window. My hands were shaking as my mind replayed the scene that had happened in my bedroom. Finally, I regained some amount of composure and turned to Denver, hesitant to trust my own voice to say the words. "Aaron forced himself on me, Denver." She immediately pulled the car over.

"What?" she exclaimed. "What do you mean he forced himself on you? Did he hit you, Angela?" Her eyes were clouded over with concern.

"No, no, no, he forced himself on me…kind of like…rape."

"What do you mean, Angela? You guys are dating! That would warrant consent, Angela." Denver looked both disturbed and confused.

"We haven't had sex before, Denver. When I got home from work, he insisted that we have sex before I went out with you."

"And what did you say?"

"I asked if we could wait until later instead of right then."

"And his response was…?"

"He wouldn't even consider it. He…he pushed me down onto the bed and…" I couldn't say the words again.

"Whatever came over him, Denver, it wasn't *Aaron*. He wasn't acting like himself at all." Tears welled up in my eyes again. I stretched the neckline of my sweater down below my shoulder to reveal where the highest scratch began.

"Whomever that was, they hurt me."

Denver gasped. "Oh Angela, you have to get away from this guy as soon as possible. He is going to hurt you worse than this one day…"

"I know, I know, that's why I had originally asked you to dinner tonight; I need your help, Denver."

"Just tell me how to help and I will," Denver said, her tone determined as she pulled back onto the road.

"Remember that doctor you dated for awhile, Mike Evans?"

"Yeah, what can he help us with?" *There's no turning back now.*

"Aaron is going to the Middle East to meet with some people from the United Nations."

"What does that have to do with Mike?"

I caught her eye as I said, "Denver, I *know* he microchipped me. I can feel it. And it's the only explanation for the control he has over me. I need Mike to take it out."

"Okay, well, if he *did* microchip you, how would he control you?"

"I have been researching online articles about microchip implants, mind control, and cybernetics. Basically, all of my research confirmed from reliable, medical sources that they have been experimenting with implanting microchips into brains for decades and you can be monitored via the microchip by a remote computer. They are barely detectable—and, as a result, difficult to remove."

"Wow, that's crazy," Denver breathed, incredulously.

"Aaron speaks frequently about Chantilly, Virginia, only twenty-four miles away from Washington D.C. The National Reconnaissance Office (N.R.O.) is stationed there, where they can control all satellites for the NSA, CIA, Air force and Navy. So, if you can get me in to see Mike as soon as Aaron's plane takes off, Mike can x-ray my neck before Aaron's plane lands. Maybe he'll even be able to remove it if it *is* in my neck. Aaron won't be able to track me while he's in the air." Denver nodded, processing everything that I had overwhelmed her with. "Denver, I just need to get the hell away from Aaron while he's still out of the country."

"Of course. When is he leaving?" Denver asked. I could almost see the wheels turning in her mind.

"Less than two weeks."

"Well, we'd better get moving on this—obviously we don't have much time."

"Thank you, Denver." I let out a deep breath and smiled at her.

"So, where shall we go for dinner?"

February 6, 2012
Goodbye and Good Riddance

Two days before Aaron was scheduled to leave, I found myself feeling anxious about my appointment with Dr. Mike Evans. Thank God for Denver, who had gone to great lengths to set it up for me. There was no doubt in my mind that he would find the microchip. I prayed constantly that he would know how to remove it once he did.

I tried my hardest not to change my behavior around Aaron, which had become especially difficult after the encounter in my bedroom. I went the extra mile two days before he was scheduled to leave; I called him from work.

"Hi baby, I know you're leaving in two days and I've been thinking…maybe we need our own getaway before you go. Would like to stay over at the Opryland Hotel tonight?" I assured myself that he couldn't detect the nervousness I felt.

"Wow, last minute, huh? I have to make a few calls first. What time are you thinking?"

"I don't know…let's plan to leave about an hour after I get out of work. Does that sound alright?"

"Yes, that sounds great, my love. I will plan to meet you at your place at six."

"Great, see you then. Bye."

As I hung up, I promised myself, *you can do this. Just make it through the next couple of days and then you will be* free*!* After leaving work early, I hurried home to pack an overnight bag. I turned on the TV for background noise, and caught up on the news. President Obama had just signed an executive order blocking all assets of the Iranian government, including the central bank, held in the United States.

Damn, I thought. Throughout the past couple of months, I had heard snippets of stories about dictators being pushed out of power in their own countries. At that moment, I realized that Aaron was right; the door was open and it wouldn't be long before the militaries of the United Nations would walk through it to set up the New World Order by force. *Aaron, who is lying low right now, will rise up to be the new world dictator, backed by the United Nation's military. As soon as they do away with the dictators, the world leaders that are considered "peaceful" will introduce Aaron as the leader of their New World. He's behind the scenes, making everything worse, so he can step forward and promise to change things for the better.* The article about the microchips came back into my mind as I continued to watch the news in horror. I wasn't really listening. I was putting the pieces together. *With the new monetary system in place, they will deceive everyone into being microchipped. Aaron will have access to private information about every soul on the planet. It's brilliant, really. Set up a supercomputer to track the citizens of the world, control the population by limiting access to their own resources, and inflict pain if they are disobedient with just a few keystrokes.*

There was no way to be sure of the reasons that Aaron was going to the Middle East, but surely it had something to do with the President's freshly signed executive order. I turned my focus back to the newscaster's words as 'BREAKING NEWS' flashed across the screen. An earthquake measuring a 7.8 on the Richter Scale had hit the Philippines. "This is the third earthquake to hit the Philippines this week," he announced. *What? How is that possible?*

I grabbed my tablet and typed 'earthquake' into a search engine. Sure enough, research confirmed that it was only the third week of January, but the number of earthquakes worldwide for 2012 already numbered a little over seven hundred worldwide—and most of them were over a 4.5, some even reaching as high as the one that was just reported on the news.

Disbelief overcame me and I sank onto the sofa. I had been so consumed with getting away from Aaron that I hadn't even been paying attention to what was going on worldwide. I felt sick to my stomach as I thought about the predictions the Bible had made about the End of Time. The earthquakes were just another sign that those things were quickly coming to pass. Trembling, I reached for the Bible on my coffee table. It had been weeks since I had opened it. I searched the index for the word "earthquake." I found a reference to earthquakes in the book of Matthew, chapter twenty-four, where Jesus said, "You will be hearing of wars and rumors of wars. See that you are not frightened, for those things must take place, but that is not yet the end. For nations will rise against nations, and kingdoms against kingdoms, and in various places there will be famines and earthquakes. But all these things are merely the beginning of birth pangs. Then, they will deliver you to tribulations, and will kill you, and you will be hated by all nations for My name."

I suddenly remembered the time and glanced at the clock. It was quarter to six. *Shit! Aaron will be here in fifteen minutes.* I hurriedly put my tablet and my Bible away. *Face it, Angela—you're nuts. You are in love with the Antichrist; you have to get away from him.* As if on cue, my phone rang with a text from Aaron.

'On my way, love. See you in a few. By the way, I'm picking up some cocaine for tonight.' *He knows I hate that shit, so why does he do it?* The use of drugs and alcohol in excess always screamed a weak person looking to escape reality, at least in my opinion. *Aaron constantly claims to live by a code, but from what I can see, his code leads to nothing but self-destruction. Although, I would probably want to numb myself from reality if I knew that I was destined to become the Antichrist.* Aaron was going to Hell for eternity, so it made sense that he would do whatever he wanted while he was on Earth. But then, I realized that he could still make a different choice.

Surely Aaron has a freewill. Maybe I should stay...I could help him fight this...

"No!" I told myself aloud, shaking the thought from my head.

'I will be there in two minutes.'

I dropped my overnight bag by the door and went over my mental checklist to make sure I had everything I needed. Aaron's voice drifted toward the door as he ascended the steps. As he opened the door, I could tell he was finishing a conversation with his personal assistant. "Send the black armored Escalade for me. My jet cannot arrive any later than ten in the morning. Tell my driver to be a few minutes early, just in case I happen to arrive sooner than I expected. See you in a few days." He hung up the phone, crossed the living room to me, and kissed my cheek softly. "Are you ready, Angela?"

"Definitely."

"We are going to have fun, Angela! Let the party begin. We'll stop on the way to get you a bottle of wine since you *hate* my cocaine."

"Okay, just make it a Chardonnay and I'll be good." I said with a wink. It felt strange to try to be charming in the very presence of a man whose love was a double-edged sword.

"We need to enjoy tonight since I'll be leaving in two days." *Two very* long *days*, I thought to myself.

We checked into the hotel and Aaron immediately made us drinks. He got out his bag of coke and placed it on the end table. As he cut out a line, he looked up at me and asked, "Are you sure you don't want to try some? It can be a fun night in bed."

I watched him snort his line and said, "Nah, I'll pass." There would be *nothing* fun about anything that followed.

February 8, 2012
Today is the Day

The day that Aaron boarded his jet at ten o'clock sharp, bound for the Middle East, I breathed a sigh of relief. I knew I had to move quickly; I was afraid he would still find a way to track me, even in the air. His schedule sounded so packed with his "clients" that I hoped he'd be too busy to worry about me.

I gave him no reason to think that I would leave him. I should have been given an Academy Award for my performance while we were together. But I had to remember that I was dealing with someone who was not a normal human being, someone who had probably microchipped me. I found myself wondering for the thousandth time, *Why me? Did God choose me for some sort of mission?*

My greatest struggle was against the feelings I had for Aaron. Part of me wanted so badly to stay with him, but another part of me held fast to the reality that he would eventually kill me because of where my ultimate loyalties where. I was a child of God. Aaron would not spare anyone who believed in God, not even the woman he claimed to love. A theory I hadn't considered embedded itself into my brain. *What if I feel this way about him because of the microchip? When it comes out, maybe these feelings will go away...*

My grip on reality seemed to be slipping away. My thoughts and feelings seemed downright *insane* and if a psychiatrist could read my mind, I would be placed in an institution. But after being around Aaron Stone, hearing his conversations, witnessing the monstrous things he did...I knew I was absolutely sane, but if I stayed with him much longer, I wouldn't be.

'Love, my jet is about to take off, I'll call you when I land.'

Even though I felt a pang of sadness, relief was the feeling that washed over me when I received the text I'd been waiting for.

'Okay, have a safe flight; I'll talk to you soon.' I waited about two hours before I shot Denver a text.

'Hey, it's Angela. Aaron left about two hours ago. Have you spoken to Dr. Evans yet today?'

'Yes I did,' she texted back.

'Great, I'll pick you up around six and we'll grab a drink.'

I hopped into my car and headed over to Denver's later that evening. Paranoid that he'd hired someone to follow me, I found myself glancing in the rearview mirror repeatedly. *Relax, Angela, no one is following you*, I reassured myself. *God, I just want this microchip out of me! I want to feel free again.*

When I arrived at her driveway, Denver was already waiting outside. She hopped into the car wearing Buckle jeans, with her black Coach bag in tow.

"Hi! I bet you feel so relieved right now!"

"I don't know, part of me is, but part of me feels strangely sad. If Dr. Evans finds that microchip and is able to remove it, then that means today was the last time I will ever see Aaron. Denver, I know it sounds crazy, but I do love him."

"I know it must be difficult for you, Angela, but you *have* to do this. Mike Evans is an amazing doctor. I have faith in him. Trust me, if anyone is able to find the chip, it'll be him. We have an appointment tomorrow at eleven thirty. I'll just pick you up at your place."

"Thanks, Denver. You're such a good friend—I really do appreciate all of your help." Denver smiled and rubbed my shoulder.

"Listen, let's not worry about it until tomorrow morning. You need a distraction…want to head to downtown Nashville for dinner?"

"Sounds perfect. I am so *freaking* hungry!"

After dinner, Denver and I stopped by Kaitlin's house to let her in on what we had planned for the following day. Denver and Kaitlin were the only two people I could fully trust. Once I realized how dangerous Aaron could be, I had made sure to keep Nick out of our lives. It was painful, but I had to protect him. I worried constantly about Aaron going after my family. *Hopefully Dr. Evans can remove this chip. But once Aaron realizes he can't track me anymore, I'm sure he'll come after me. I need to warn Nick…*

Denver and I pulled up to Kaitlin's house. We smiled at each other. I was confident that between the three of us, we could create the perfect escape plan. After ringing Kaitlin's doorbell, I paused on her doorstep, staring across the street at the house Kyle and I had shared before our divorce. I briefly allowed my mind to wander back to the times that Kyle and I had shared, wondering about how things might have been different had he not left me.

"Angela? Are you coming in or what?" Kaitlin's voice cut through my bittersweet thoughts.

"Sorry about that; I was just daydreaming about my old life."

"Well, you better get in here and figure out your *new* life." Kaitlin and Denver looked at each other and laughed.

"Ha ha, really funny you two," I retorted. I was surprised to hear genuine amusement in my own words. My relief was cut short when I stepped through the door and my phone rang. "Shhhhh, it's Aaron!" I exclaimed. They immediately went silent.

"Hi baby," I answered with casual excitement. "You got there fast!"

"Well, we made a pit stop in Washington D.C., so we're not in the Middle East yet." *Oh, shit*, I thought, realizing that he had probably been tracking me.

"I have a federal bank meeting with a few private investors first, and then from here I will be flying out of the country," he continued. "By the way, tell Denver and Kaitlin I said hello and to take good care of you." I could detect his arrogance on the other end of the line.

"Sure thing, baby," I said cheerfully, trying to keep my cool. I couldn't let on how terrified I was.

"I have to go, love. My meeting starts in ten minutes." He hung up.

"Angela...what did he say? Your face is *white!*" Kaitlin remarked. I explained what was going on, while my mind formulated a plan.

"If Dr. Evans finds and removes the microchip, I have two choices. One, I can stay here and wait for Aaron to return. I could deceive him into thinking that the microchip is malfunctioning. I could try to *stop* him...or, I could pack up my shit tomorrow and get the hell out of here."

Denver and Kaitlin exchanged glances, and Denver spoke.

"Why don't we wait until we see Dr. Evans and then make a decision?" Kaitlin nodded.

"There's no sense in getting worked up until we know all of our options." I was near tears, but I nodded in agreement.

"Until then, just play it cool if Aaron calls you," Kaitlin continued. "Make sure that you tell him you're going to the doctor with Denver tomorrow. If he *is* tracking you, being honest with him will keep him from being suspicious."

"Yes, that's a great idea Kaitlin." She reached for my hand.

"Let's all pray, Angela. Everything is going to be fine."

After some prayer and a couple cups of coffee, Denver and I said our goodbyes to Kaitlin and left. The drive back to Denver's was quiet. Before she got out of the car, Denver turned to me, "I know this is hard on you, Angela. Things might be tough for a while, but I believe that they will get *much* better. In time, God will work all of this out for you." I felt tears well up in my eyes.

"You know, Denver, the other side of what Aaron says about the New World Order and his being the Antichrist, is that the Bible says Christ is coming back soon. Christ is supposed to come back for his believers, the ones who trust in His name, before the Antichrist comes into power. So, maybe I won't have to worry about any of this." Denver patted my arm gently.

"All we need to do is believe. I will see you tomorrow, Angela." As I watched Denver walk up her driveway and into her house, I felt overwhelmed and uncertain about what my future held. One thing I was sure about was that I was grateful for my sweet, brave friends.

February 9, 2012
Doctor, Doctor

At nine o'clock the next morning, I received a text from Denver saying that she would pick me up in an hour so we could head over to Dr. Evans's office. After texting back a quick response, I hopped into the shower. My hands were shaking as I applied my makeup. Nervous shudders racked my body. Anticipation was taking over—mixed with confusion and crippling fear. Important decisions had to be made and time was of the essence.

This new path I knew I was headed for was sure to be fearful and lonely. That was the worst part, knowing that I would be all alone. I was scared to death. And the romantic irony of it all was that I would be trying to outrun the very man I wanted nothing more than to run toward. My phone beeped.

'Be there in five.'

'Meet you downstairs,' I replied.

I threw on a pair of jeans, grabbed my white sneakers, and headed out the door. I was about halfway down the stairs when I realized I had forgotten to grab my purse. I turned around and trudged back up the stairs. The second I stepped back through my apartment door, my phone rang. Thinking it was Denver asking about my abrupt about-face, I pulled my phone out of my pocket.

"Hello?"

It was Aaron. "Hey baby." *Oh no, what do I say? Why is he calling me now? Regroup...remember what Kaitlin said...you have to throw off his suspicion.* "Angela," he said impatiently.

"Hey, baby," I answered, "Sorry, you were cutting out."

"Oh, I see. Well, what are you up to?"

"I'm with Denver. We are on our way to go see her doctor," I said coolly.

"Why? What's wrong with Denver?" *Do I hear concern or skepticism in his voice?*

"Oh, nothing," I said quickly. "It's the doctor who she is dating. We are just going to stop by to visit." I giggled in an attempt to make my story sound more credible.

"Ah, okay," he seemed distracted.

I continued, hoping to convince him, "You know Denver...it's like a new guy every week with her."

We both laughed at that comment and I felt relief. Surely he believed me.

"What's this doctor boyfriend's name?" Aaron inquired.

"Dr. Evans..." I said, a little apprehensively. *Either I tell him now or he finds out when he tracks me.*

"Hmmmm, Evans. Never heard of him. All right, I'll let you go. I was just calling to say I love you and that I'll be busy for the next few days. I promise to text you in between my meetings, though."

"Okay, baby, good luck with your meetings," I replied cheerily.

"Bye, love." And with that, we hung up.

I'd ignored the flash of my phone during our entire conversation, and sure enough, when I opened my texts, I had three from Denver. I chuckled to myself, as they were all basically different renditions of 'Hey, I am downstairs waiting for you.'

This time I remembered my purse as I left my apartment and made my way down the stairs. I opened the car door and smiled a greeting to Denver.

"Hey."

"Hi! What took so long? Didn't you see my texts?" she asked, her tone more puzzled than miffed.

"Sorry, I ran back up for my purse and Aaron called."

"Ohhh…everything okay?"

"Yeah, he was just calling to say hi. I told him I was going with you to the doctor's office. He wanted to know the doctor's name, so I told him. He said he's never heard of Dr. Evans though, thank God!"

"Well that's good, I suppose," said Denver, a hint of uncertainty in her voice.

"Hopefully Dr. Evans will find this chip," I returned, wistfully.

Twenty minutes later, we pulled into the parking lot. An uncomfortable sensation slithered up my neck. *Is Aaron tracking me already? Or, is the interference from all of the electric equipment in Dr. Evans's office?*

I wasn't quite sure what caused the sensation; I only knew that something had set off that microchip. The sensation increased in intensity as we walked toward the door. We strode straight up to the receptionist's desk, gave her my name, and made ourselves as comfortable as we could in the waiting room's chairs. There were only a handful of other people in the room, but it was eerily quiet. I could hear the pounding of my own heartbeat.

I gazed past the other brown furniture in the waiting room and on a table to the left a pile of magazines caught my eye. The title of one headline on the cover of the topmost magazine read, "This Is the Year of the Antichrist." Suddenly, I felt faint. Denver's voice cut through my thoughts.

"Angela? Are you okay? Snap out of it you look as if you've seen a ghost." I smiled over at Denver, thankful that she was beside me.

"I'm just nervous."

"Try not to worry about it. We've made it this far. It's all downhill from here." She reached out for my hand and I gave hers a small squeeze in appreciation. I couldn't bring down the supportive vibes by telling her about the sensations I was feeling in my neck. Denver stood up and walked over to the magazines. She picked up the top one, read the headline, and quickly rifled through the others in the glossy pile.

A wave of desolation washed over me at the thought of Aaron, along with that ever-present feeling of fear. I missed him. I knew that deep down I didn't want to leave him. However, I had no choice. My life was hanging in the balance between good and evil, right and wrong, love and hate, God and Satan. *These feelings are all technically self-inflicted, but I am only human, after all.*

"Angela? Angela Russo?" a voice permeated my thoughts. I looked up and saw a slender, redheaded nurse cradling a clipboard, looking around for a response.

"That's us," I said as I turned to Denver.

She smiled and put down her magazine. We stood up and the nurse motioned for us to follow her. She led us down a long hallway and opened a door to a small room with a large, blue x-ray table sitting in the center. Two plastic chairs sat against the wall in the corner of the tiny room.

"Dr. Evans will be with you shortly," the nurse told us reassuringly before she closed the door behind her.

"Cross your fingers," I whispered to Denver. She lifted up her hands to show me that her fingers were, in fact, already crossed, and we giggled nervously. The rest of the waiting period elapsed in silence after what felt like hours. The ticking of the clock echoed off the walls and I took deep breaths of the sterile air. Finally, we heard footsteps and the doorknob turning as Dr. Evans entered the room. A dark-haired man of average height and a ruddy complexion greeted us.

"Hello, Angela, I am Dr. Evans. Denver has told me a lot about you." I got up to shake his hand, and as I turned toward him, I noticed that his eyes were a radiant sky blue—a color that had me reminiscing about my younger years.

I was born into a family of five children. My father succumbed to a heart attack at the age of forty-one, leaving behind four children and a wife who was eight months pregnant at the time. Life for my family was not the neat, orderly house with green grass and a white picket fence out of a picturesque fantasy. My older brother was killed in a motorcycle accident a few years after my father's death; as a result, my mother was left caring for three little girls and a toddling little boy. The one thing I would never forget about my older brother, though, were his eyes. They were a brilliant sky blue.

Looking into the eyes of Dr. Evans was just like looking into those eyes that comforted me for years as a young girl. This time it wasn't my brother, but a man that might be the key to my freedom, and I found at ease in that sight again.

"Nice to meet you, Dr. Evans," I replied to his greeting.

"So Denver told me a little bit about what's going on, but would you mind filling me in?"

"I believe I have a microchip in my neck," I answered, getting straight to the point.

"Well, Angela, microchips can be quite difficult to detect. Sometimes the glass encapsulated RFID chips are injected deep into the patient's flesh. This tag can be read by radio waves from a few inches away. Once limited to tracking cattle, these tags are now used to track vehicles, airline passengers, Alzheimer's patients, pets, and they will soon be tracking groceries worldwide as well. The endgame is that these RFID tags will communicate with an electronic reader, so they can send information about a purchased product to the manufacturer, who will, in turn, notify your bank, and as a result, an amount equal to the grocery bill will be deducted from your bank account. It is, essentially, grocery shopping of the future."

"That's brilliant," Denver remarked. "No lines, no waiting."

"Yes, but as I said, they are difficult to detect and remove unless you have the right equipment, which is why you've come to the right place." He turned toward one of the machines, with confidence in his voice as he continued, "This measures the electromagnetic field meter, or EMF, of the microchip, and from that measurement I am able to detect the radio frequency identification, or RFID, that is used. This biometric technology is used for security by microchip delivery."

"If it is detected, can you remove it, Dr. Evans?" I asked, riveted by this new and complicated sounding process.

"I will not be completely certain until we are able to locate the microchip. Once I have located it, I must assess whether or not the area is operable. There are areas where I cannot operate—it can be especially dangerous if the chip is implanted in the vicinity of the nervous system. If worse comes to worse, we can look into deactivating the microchip as a safer alternative." I shifted uncomfortably and his voice softened.

"Denver told me all about Aaron, Angela. He will be able to recognize the lack of radio waves if I take the chip out. But if I deactivate the tag, he might just assume that there is a malfunction, and chances are, he won't suspect you've done anything to tamper with it. You must understand, though, that we are still in the testing phase of deactivation. We have discovered that the chips can *already* be used as a payment instrument when associated with credit cards and pre-paid accounts. Angela, they're preparing to do away with a physical form of currency. It is amazing what they can do these days, Angela. Technology has become so damn advanced. But the government restricts our abilities to properly research these things. One day, that *will* end," Dr. Evans explained, his tone wistful.

I looked over at Denver and she offered me a reassuring smile. I took a deep breath, smiled back at her, and turned my attention again to Dr. Evans.

"Okay, let's do this," I replied, mustering up as much enthusiasm as I could.

February 9, 2012 (continued)
The Operation

Alone with my thoughts and the hum of the fan in the ladies' room, I stared at my reflection. As instructed, I had changed into the thin, flower-patterned hospital gown and pulled my hair up off of my neck. The lighting was poor, which made my worried face look far paler than it should have.

I was afraid of everything—afraid Dr. Evans wouldn't find the microchip. Afraid he wouldn't be able to remove it. Afraid that if he did, Aaron would find out. And who knew what Aaron would do then…

Shaking, I walked back into the examination room with my clothes in hand. Dr. Evans and Denver hushed their conversation as I sat down. "Angela, I'm going to have you lay on your stomach, so I can scan your neck for images of the RFID. We'll give you a sedative, so you shouldn't feel anything, but you may feel a warm, tingling sensation. There will be no discomfort during this procedure."

I nodded that I understood, anxious to have validation for my sanity. "Once I locate the chip, I will measure its proximity from your spinal cord. Ideally, we would just deactivate a chip by placing it in a microwave on high for five seconds. Obviously, we can't place you in a microwave," he chuckled, probably trying to lighten the mood. Denver and I exchanged glances and he continued.

"Hopefully, the chip is far enough away from your spinal cord that we can operate. If not, our options become less ideal, but we *do* still have options. There are ways to pierce the microchip to interfere with its ability to properly transmit a signal. Or, I can attach a piece of metal to the microchip that will block its frequency. These procedures can be painful, unfortunately, and they are not always guaranteed to be one-hundred-percent effective."

"Whatever we need to do—you're the doctor," I said with what I thought was a confident smile. Dr. Evans turned his gaze toward Denver.

"Maybe you should wait outside the door while we use the RFID machine," he suggested. Denver nodded and offered me a brave smile.

"I think that's a good idea. It will be over before you know it, Angela." She squeezed my hand and wished me good luck. Dr. Evans followed her out of the room.

While they were both gone, I slipped off my shoes and stood. The concrete was cold beneath my bare feet. Chills ran up my spine and throughout my body. I could feel the hairs on the back of my neck stand up. I sighed deeply, closed my eyes, and bowed my head.

Well, God, my fate is in your hands. Whatever your will is for me, I know that you are in control.

I heard footsteps in the hallway. Dr. Evans entered the room with the redheaded nurse on his heels. "Angela, are you ready?" I nodded and the nurse quietly closed the door. "This is LeAnn," Dr. Evans introduced her. "She's going to give you a sedative to relax you. It's very important that you remain calm and still during this procedure."

As I clambered up onto the table, the nurse walked over to administer the shot. I felt a slight pinch from the needle in my arm and seconds later I could already feel the effects of the sedative coursing through my body. Dr. Evans seemed far away as he asked, "Angela, can you hear me? Angela?" as I felt myself drifting off…

The next thing I remember, I looked up to see the redheaded nurse smiling at me. "How do you feel, Angela? We are finished; you did great! Take a few minutes to get your bearings. You may get up and get dressed as soon as you feel up to it. Dr. Evans will be in to speak with you in a few minutes."

As I became more lucid, I sat up, still feeling a little groggy. I slid off the table and staggered over to my folded clothes on the counter. Soon after I was dressed, there was a discreet knock on the door. "Angela, are you dressed?" It wasn't Dr. Evans's voice that came from the other side of the door. It was Denver.

"Yes, come in," I said, anxious to see my friend. Denver gave me a big hug.

"How do you feel?"

"Groggy," I admitted with a shrug.

"Yeah, sedatives will do that to you," said Denver with a laugh.

"Did he find it, Denver? Do you know if he found it?" I asked, shamelessly hopeful. She looked at me, smiled, and nodded her head forward slightly. Relief washed over me, erasing the last bit of grogginess.

"Oh my God, I can't believe that it's out!" I exclaimed.

"Angela, he didn't take it out," she responded, hesitantly. "He was able to deactivate it, but…well, just let him explain what he did."

When Dr. Evans made his appearance, he smiled at me and asked, "Angela, are you feeling alright?"

"I'm feeling a lot better now, though I felt a bit groggy earlier."

"Well, that's to be expected. I assume that Denver has told you the good news—I did indeed find the microchip. It was very close to your vertebrae, though. I did not risk attempting to remove it. I made a small incision next to it and was able to deactivate the tag. So, as of about thirty or so minutes ago, it is no longer transmitting to the reader."

At that point, I was just happy to have the microchip deactivated. It would allow me enough time to figure out my next move before Aaron returned from the Middle East.

After finishing up some paperwork, I thanked Dr. Evans profusely for what he did for me. As I walked out the door to where

Denver was waiting in the car, I realized that for the first time in a long time, I finally felt free. I should have known it wouldn't last long.

February 10, 2012
On the Run

Although the first victory was deactivating the chip, I only had a few days to implement a plan and put it into action. I knew I needed to get in touch with Nick. I had to warn him. He would be the first person Aaron would question and we needed to be on the same page when it came to the story of my whereabouts.

Nick's number was in my favorites list. I felt a pang of guilt as I hit the call button; it had been too long since I had called him. Waiting for Nick to pick up, I thought back to that last conversation Nick and I had about Aaron Stone. *Why didn't I listen to Nick back then? I was so blinded by Aaron's affection—my own son was trying to warn me and I couldn't even see it!* On the other end of the line, I heard Nick's voice as he picked up, "Hi, Mom, what's up?"

"Hi, honey, can we talk?"

"Sure."

"In person? Maybe over some coffee?"

"Yeah, sure, Ma. Is Starbrew good? In about half an hour?"

"That's perfect," I answered. "I'll see you in thirty."

After I hung up, I began to gather the essentials for my escape. I unlocked the wooden chest in my bedroom that contained all of my important documents. I reached inside and pulled out my passport, the title to my car, and my bank account information. I grabbed my purple backpack out of my closet and shoved all of the papers into it. *I can't forget my jewelry!* I realized. *I can sell it if I need more money.*

After placing the last of my jewelry into the backpack, I glanced at my watch. It was time to leave to meet Nick. I pulled the backpack over my shoulder and headed down the stairs.

The five-minute drive to Starbrew felt shorter than usual as I pulled into a spot right beside Nick's car. We got out of our cars and Nick gave me a big hug.

I really needed that hug. Although I wanted to break down and cry at the thought of this possibly being the last time I would ever get to see my son, I knew I needed to stay cool and collected. *Don't let Nick see you lose your composure, Angela.*

"You okay, Mom?"

"I am fine, honey. I just made some important decisions in my life that I want you to know about," I replied, still uncertain how much I should tell him. *I just need to tell him the truth.*

We headed over to a little table tucked into the corner, as far out of earshot as we could be from the other customers. Nick dropped his keys on the table and asked, "Ma, what can I get you?"

"A caramel macchiato is good, honey. Just a small one, please."

While Nick waited in line to give our order to the barista, I went over in my head what I would say to him. My mind was practically screaming, *Tell him the truth!*

I was afraid to tell him the truth because I knew it would sound completely absurd. How could I tell my son that I'd fallen in love with the Antichrist, he had microchipped me, and I was now on the run from him? How could I put the pieces of conversations I'd overheard together in a way that he would understand? Aaron had told me so much, but there was still a lot I didn't know.

There was no telling how long it would be before Aaron figured out what I had done. I hoped that his meetings in the Middle East kept him distracted long enough for me to hide. I shivered at the thought of the man I loved hunting me down like a wild animal.

I glanced up as Nick placed my caramel macchiato on the table in front of me. "Here, Ma, I told them extra whipped cream, just the way you like it."

"Thank you, honey."

As I reached for my coffee, I could see my hand shaking. Tears sprang into my eyes.

"Are you okay, Mom? You're shaking." Nick looked concerned. "What's wrong?"

"I have to tell you something, Nick, and I need you to promise me that you'll believe me, no matter how crazy it sounds."

"Go ahead; I promise I'll believe you," he responded. My baby boy's eyes were intense as he leaned forward.

"Okay, I don't know the best way to explain what's happened, Nick, but here goes nothing. Aaron is in the Middle East, as we speak, having secret meetings with the heads of the United Nations. I know that he's been drafting plans for strategic military placement all over the world to implement the New World Order. He's planning to replace the world's currency with a digitalized economic system, called The BEAST, which stands for the Banking and Economic Analytics System Tracker. Everyone will be tagged, like cattle, with microchips that can be read through their radio frequencies by a supercomputer at anytime. I know this might sound like science fiction to you, Nick, but all of it is true. He'll promise the world that he is going to save them, but his real agenda is to unite the alien races from which he originated. The world will be deceived. They'll accept the BEAST and the microchips, or he will kill them. Once he sets his plan in motion, it will be impossible to purchase anything without a chip: gas, food, water..." I could see Nick's eye growing wide.

"Aaron's New World Order basically means he will have complete control over the entire population, from birth to death."

The wheels were turning in Nick's head. "So, how do we stop him?"

"Nick, I don't know if we can. Aaron put a chip in me to track me. I just went to a doctor and had it deactivated, but I need to find a place to hide in case he comes after me."

"Wow," Nick was shocked. "We have to get you out of here. Where are you thinking about going?"

"I've been thinking about New York. Aaron would probably assume that I'd go to New Jersey, Florida, or California…the places where most of my friends and family are. He knows I hate New York City, so he'd never think to look there. The city that never sleeps has a population of nine million, so it should be easy to hide in plain sight."

Nick nodded somberly. "That makes sense. You know my brothers are out there, Dante and Mario? We'll get you in touch with them as soon as you get there. I'll call them when I get in the car. Do you remember where the boathouse is in Central Park?"

"I think so."

"I'll tell them to meet you there. I can stay here to act as a decoy when Aaron gets back." The thought of that monster coming after my son terrified me.

"Nick, just be careful. Aaron is a very dangerous man. I wish I had never fallen in love with him…" Nick's eyes softened, but his expression was determined.

"Don't worry about what's already passed. We need to stay focused on a plan." I blinked back my tears and nodded. I knew he was right.

"Ma, you need to buy a pre-paid phone. Download an app for the Dragon Fire game. Send me a friend request. My screen name is NickRusso with no space. Once you add me, we can chat privately through the game. Make up a name that has nothing to do with yours. Aaron won't be able to track our conversations." I shook my head, completely amazed. My son had grown into such a brilliant, sweet man. I was so proud of him.

"That's a great idea, Nick. Aaron doesn't really know about your brothers, but I'm sure he'll do some digging and send people after them. Make sure you use someone else's phone if you try to contact them. Should he pull up your phone records, you don't want him tracing their location. Once he realizes that my microchip is no longer transmitting, which he may have already done, he'll try to find me. When he can't get ahold of me, all hell will break loose. I have no idea what he will do in retaliation, but my fear is that he will come after you. I don't want you to stay here any longer than you need to. Aaron is capable of a lot of terrible things. He's not an ordinary man. The spirit of Lucifer lives inside of him. We're up against a dark, evil force—the Antichrist." Nick reached across the table and squeezed my hand.

"Mom, you taught me that God is the Creator of all things. He's *always* in control of our situation, no matter how bad it looks. You need to believe your own words now more than ever."

February 11, 2012
New York City

I arrived home for what I knew would be the last time. As I finished packing up the essentials for my getaway, I heard the phone ring. I grabbed it off the table and saw that it was Denver. "Hey, Denver!" I answered, breathless from rushing around my apartment. Unexpectedly, Denver's voice was hysterical on the other end of the line. I couldn't make anything out through the sounds of her cries. "Denver! What's wrong?"

Her words were almost indistinguishable, but what I could understand made my blood run cold.

"Bomb! Bomb! He killed them all...Oh my God, Angela! He killed them all!"

"What the hell are you talking about, Denver? I need you to calm down because I don't get what you're trying to tell me." I could hear her taking shallow breaths as she tried to regain some sense of composure. A few moments later, her words came through hiccups.

"There was an explosion...at Dr. Evans's office. No survivors."

"What?" I reached for my remote and flipped to the local news. The images I saw were the smoldering remains of the office I had been in just one day earlier. "Oh my God, Denver! You need to get out of your house! Go somewhere safe! Get the hell out of there! NOW!"

A deafening explosion on the other end of the line cut her response and the phone went silent. "DENVER!" I screamed. "DENVER!" It felt like someone had ripped my heart out of my chest. Her face flashed through my mind and I knew my friend was gone. Falling to my knees, I took deep breaths, trying to remain conscious. *Angela*, my mind beckoned, *you have to pull it together. You've got to get out of here. He's coming for you.*

Somehow, I pulled myself off of my living room floor. It was time to go. There was only one thing left to do. In case Aaron tried to trace my phone, I had to leave it at home. I ripped a piece of paper off of my refrigerator and grabbed a pen from my table. I scribbled every important contact listed in my cell phone doing my best to ignore the nausea I felt when I passed over Denver's name.

Just as I laid my phone down on the table and took one last look around, I heard it ring. I raced over, hoping that by some miracle, it would be Denver. When I saw the name, my stomach dropped. *Holy shit, it's Aaron!* As I picked up the phone, knowing I had to answer, it felt like someone was twisting a knife into my abdomen. *Angela, he can't know that you know about the bombing.*

"Hello," I answered, as calmly as I possibly could.

"Hi, love." *Hi, love. Really? This monster has the audacity to be nonchalant? Okay, two can play this game.*

"Hey baby, how's work?" I laid the sweetness on thick, dragging "baby" out.

"Great, the business is finished, so now it's all play. I will be flying home tomorrow."

"Oh, I can't wait to see you," I lied.

"How did everything go with Denver the other day?" The fact that he even said her name sent chills up my spine. I was shaking.

"Everything went well. Thank you for asking about her. Your concern for my friends means so much to me, Aaron." He was silent. "You know," I continued, "I should probably give her a call at some point today."

"Oh, I would imagine you will be hearing from Denver sooner or later, Angela." *I hate Aaron Stone*, I seethed on the inside. "And you will most certainly see me soon. I miss you so much, my love. Have you missed me?"

"Of course, Aaron."

The funny thing was, up until that point, I had missed him. I'd almost been grieving the end of our relationship, replaying the fun memories we'd shared. But now, now that I knew what he had done, I just wanted to give him pain that he had inflicted upon me. I wanted him to come back and be heartbroken when he couldn't find me. I wanted his love for me to turn to hatred, just as my love for him had.

"Well, before you know it, we will be together."

"Not soon enough," I responded, my enthusiasm sprouting from my anger.

"Aw, you are so sweet to me," he said, chuckling with amusement. *Surely he knows that I know. How could he not?*

"Almost as sweet as you, baby. I'll see you soon."

"Goodbye, Angela." I couldn't hang up fast enough. 'Breaking News' flashed across the screen and I turned the volume off of mute with the remote.

"Just after the bombing at the office of Doctor Mike Evans in Brentwood, there have been two more explosions in the Franklin area, at residences belonging to Denver Minks and Kaitlin Baker. The FBI is investigating a possible connection to these bombings and the one that occurred at Dr. Evans's facility."

It felt like my heart had stopped beating as I hung on every word the reporter said. "At this time, only one body has been found. Forty-seven-year-old Kaitlin Baker has been pronounced dead. Investigators are still searching the remains of Denver Minks's residence for her body." *Oh my God! Oh my God!* I fell to my knees, crying. *Look what I've done! If I hadn't gotten them involved, they would still be alive.* I started pounding my fist into the floor, yelling, "How can I ever forgive myself? All of this is my fault!" The tears stung my eyes and burned my tongue as I screamed over and over, "God, where the hell are you? Why are you letting this happen?"

His voice came instantly. It was still and quiet, but I heard it. *"Angela. I am still in control. I know you do not understand your present circumstances, but very soon, you will. From this day on, I will open your eyes to all of the demonic forces that surround you. I will give you the insight and ability to know whether or not the human vessels you come into contact with are being controlled by evil. I will blind their eyes and open yours, so you will see them for who they are, but they will not know who you are."* I opened my eyes, sensing His presence, but I couldn't see Him. *"Listen to Me, Angela: you are not safe here. You must leave at once!"*

Suddenly, a bright white light flashed before my eyes and surrounded my body like a bubble. A sensation I can only describe as an electric shock ran through me. I knew instantly that I was a human being having a divine experience. My body had previously felt weak, but I gradually felt myself strengthening. A warm peace rushed through my freezing, shaking body. It was as if my Maker was passing His strength and peace on to me. Every fear I'd had evaporated and it was as though a shot of adrenaline surged through me. I pulled myself off of the floor, placed my phone on the coffee table, picked up my belongings and headed out the door. With a fifteen-hour drive to New York City ahead of me, I fired up my engine and took one last glance at my apartment building. There wasn't an ounce of fear left in me as I backed out of that parking space. I wasn't the same Angela.

February 11, 2012 (continued)
On the Road

Several miles down the highway, I took an exit to buy a prepaid phone at a gas station. I made sure to get one that had Internet access so I could contact Nick and check the news. I made sure to use cash, the only untraceable exchange for the commodities I needed.

Once back on the road, I began to think of a new alias. I had a better chance of hiding from Aaron and whatever cronies he would send after me if I had some sort of a disguise and a false background.

For such a time as this, the quote from the book of Esther came to mind. I had studied her a few years earlier and was amazed by her story. She was an amazing woman—her strength and courage made her a warrior princess for God. I'd heard its aid that character qualities were often hidden in a name, so I hoped that if I borrowed her name, I could absorb those traits. So from then on, my name would be Esther.

I pulled my new phone off of the car charger as soon as it was ready and pulled up the local news. I was on edge, anxious for any news about Denver. Within seconds, I found what I was looking for, but to my dismay, there was no new information. They still hadn't found Denver's body, which made me hopeful that she was still alive. *Please protect my friend,* I prayed silently.

With a lonely fifteen-hour drive ahead of me, I turned on the radio and tried to distract myself by listening to the lyrics. Four hours into the drive, a love song came onto the radio and I couldn't keep myself from reminiscing about my relationship with Aaron. *Why me?* I wondered for the thousandth time. It was the one question that had haunted me every single day that I'd spent with Aaron. *What is so important about* me *that Lucifer incarnate needs me in his life?*

Driving down the road with those thoughts, I remembered Sarah Connor from *The Terminator*. Although I wasn't trying to save the world from a nuclear explosion, I felt like I could relate to her. I had a special mission; I had to stay focused.

A few more hours passed and I needed to stop for gas. My legs had cramped up and were aching for a good stretch. I pulled into a gas station in Trenton, New Jersey, and an attendant with a helpful smile approached my car. "Can you please fill it with premium?" I asked him, with my driver's side window cracked just a couple of inches.

While the attendant filled my gas tank, I wandered over to the convenience store. Coffee was essential if I was to stay awake for the rest of my drive. As I opened the door, I noticed three men waiting in line to make their purchases and a sudden sensation ran through my body. It was as if an electrical pulse surged from my core to my limbs. I sensed danger the moment I stepped inside and the thick stench of sulfur filled the air, making me sick to my stomach. One of the men who had been speaking to the clerk, turned around to look at the man behind him. *Holy cow!*

I was taken aback by what I saw: his eyes were a bright red, as if they were glowing. *Oh my God, not again!* The way his eyes glowed was identical to the way I had seen Aaron's eyes glow. I knew I had to get out of there. As quickly as I could, I returned to my car and handed a wad of cash to the attendant.

"Everything o—?" answered the confused attendant. With a smile I rolled up my window cutting off his question. I fired up my engine and took off immediately. *Was that what the voice meant when it told me it would let me see the demonic forces?* It made sense. Maybe God had opened my eyes so that I could walk away unharmed. I had no other protection from the demons, but at least I could see them. I just had to pay attention.

When I finally arrived in New York City, I was exhausted and starving. I had driven through the night and it was about ten in the morning when I pulled my car into a space across from Central Park. "Thank goodness I remember how to parallel park," I mumbled to myself, taking a deep breath as I surveyed my surroundings.

I unplugged my new phone from its charger so I could look through the apps. I had to find that game to download so I could communicate with Nick. I silently hoped that he had been able to contact Mario and Dante about us meeting up. Once I found the game, I downloaded it, invited Nick to chat, and waited for a response. I took a walk down the street, hoping to stumble upon some sort of breakfast café. I kept my eyes peeled for men with glowing eyes and my nose alert for the smell of sulfur. I wondered if I would ever feel truly safe again.

As I walked into a café, the hostess smiled at me. "How many in your party?" she asked me.

"One please," I answered her, feeling extremely lonely for a moment. As she escorted me to my table, I saw Dante and Mario sitting in a booth toward the right side of the café.

"Excuse me, Miss, I just spotted my sons in the booth over there. If you don't mind, I'd like to sit with them."

"Of course," she said sweetly.

A grin spread across Mario's face as he saw me approaching the table.

"Mom, how did you find us?" he asked, standing up to give me a hug. "We were supposed to meet at the boathouse." Dante stood up right behind him and reached out to me for a hug.

"Mom, I can't believe you're here!" he exclaimed. The loneliness I had felt five minutes before was replaced with great joy at the sight of my children. I caught them up on what was going on, but I did my best to give them the shortened version of recent events because I wasn't sure if they would quite understand.

Mario came up with a plan for us to stay at Beau's loft, which overlooks Chelsea Pier, so we would be within walking distance of everything. In a few weeks, we would find a place of our own, but at the time, it was the safest choice we could make—especially since putting our names on leases and contracts would leave a paper trail for Aaron Stone to follow.

I had forgotten how hard it was to find a parking spot in Manhattan, but thanks to the management of Beau's building, we were able to park for free. We trudged up three flights of stairs and a door opened to reveal a man with a headful of long, shaggy brown hair that could belong to only one person—Beau.

"Welcome to my place, Angela! It's so good to see you again!" Beau said, leaning over to hug me. I had always adored Beau; he and Mario had been friends since childhood. A few years ago they decided to open skateboarding shops in five locations around the city together. Dante was much younger than the two of them, but his knack for business was impeccable, so they hired him as their vice president of sales. Dante looked like a skateboarder with his long, blond hair, tall, slender stature, and big, brown eyes; needless to say, his appearance helped him sell skateboards with ease. Mario, on the other hand, was a few inches shorter with dark hair. Despite their differing physical traits, their character traits were so similar that even complete strangers would have been able to guess that they were brothers.

Looking around Beau's three-bedroom loft, I was impressed by how clean it was. "Your bedroom is over here, Angela," said Beau, smiling at me. We walked down a short, narrow hallway. The door to my room was on the right. *What a cute room!* I liked that

Beau had decorated it in soft, earthy tones. The queen-sized bed fit snugly in the corner. A flat screen sat on the dresser and pictures of snowcapped mountains with beautiful sunsets hung on the walls, framed in a light pinewood. I laid my suitcase on the bed, and followed my nose to the kitchen.

It was not the smell of sulfur this time, but the rich aroma of coffee that drew me down the hallway. The shiny, stainless steel appliances in the kitchen were all brand new. A large island with a black granite countertop stood in the middle of the kitchen, along with three wooden stools. My cellphone beeped and I looked down at it to see that Nick had accepted my request. I messaged him via the game. 'Hey Nick, how is everything there? Any news on Aaron's return?'

Waiting for him to respond, I poured myself a cup of coffee and sat down at the island. I could hear Mario, Dante, and Beau laughing in the next room. My phone beeped with Nick's reply. 'He's back and he is very upset.'

'Are you sure? Did you get a visit from him? Any news on Denver?' I wrote back.

'Ma, he came to my house looking for you. I told him I haven't heard from you in a week. He said not to worry that you're probably with friends, and that when he finds out where you are he will let me know. To tell you the truth, nothing came up about Denver or Kaitlin. Please, Mom, be careful—he is not happy that you left without contacting him.'

'Nick, I am with your brothers at Beau's loft. Please, honey, you be careful, too. If you need me, text through this game. I'll make sure I keep the notifications on at all times. I love you, Nick, and if you feel you need to get out of there, just leave. This is very important: do NOT trust a word from Aaron's mouth, no matter what he says!'

'Okay, Ma, I promise. I love you, too. Don't worry, I'll be fine. I will keep in touch.'

* * * *

A few weeks later, I decided to go job hunting. I walked into a restaurant around the corner. As I was filling out the application, I felt unease course through my body. The unmistakable stench of sulfur permeated the air. I looked around, knowing that something evil was in the same room as me. I could feel its presence—and then I saw him walking toward me, his eyes glowing red in the darkness of the restaurant.

If he sees me, he could tell Aaron where I am! I wasn't sure how word got around in the demonic world, but I wasn't interested in waiting around to find out. Thinking quickly, I pretended to drop my pen on the floor. I bent down to pick it up off the floor just as the man walked past me. Once he disappeared into a back room, I stood up and sprinted to the door as quickly as possible.

On the way back to Beau's, I saw a busy little Italian bar with a bakery shop in it that I had never noticed before. With the intention of purchasing some cannolis, I joined the line of people waiting just outside the doors. As I got closer to the entrance of the Italian place, I saw a discreet sign in the window that read, 'Help Wanted.' As soon as I saw it, I knew that this was where I was supposed to apply. The woman who was standing at the register when I made it to the front of the line smiled at me and asked, "Can I help you?" in a cheerful voice, as though I was the only person in line.

"May I please order five cannolis…and can you tell me if the position you're hiring for has been filled yet?" I replied.

"Are you interested?" she asked. "I can get you an application."

"Yes, I am interested, so that would be great. I can even fill it out right now."

"Sure, one moment please," the woman said as she turned toward the back room. She returned a moment later with the application and a pen. Handing them to me, she said, "You can sit over there if you'd like." The table she'd gestured to was in the corner, and it was one of the few tables left. I glanced down at my watch and observed that it was only four o'clock. *This café serves only alcohol and desserts, and this place is already hopping!*

The cafe was beautifully decorated; they'd brought outside scenery inside. Large trees and mini waterfalls adorned the room, and were surrounded by a black cobblestone paved floor, scattered with white wicker tables and chairs. The zebra print umbrellas on the tables gave the place a subtle safari feel. Large, wooden frames with flowerpots hanging from them decorated the walls.

I returned my completed application to the woman and after looking it over, she said, "My name is Maggie. My husband, Michael, and I are the owners of the café. Is there a chance that you could come back tomorrow at nine-thirty for an interview?"

"Yes, Maggie, I would love to! I will see you then." I smiled as we shook hands and she gave me the box of cannolis I'd purchased earlier. My only worry on my way back to Beau's was whether Maggie and Michael would ask to see a photo ID or my Social Security card. I had listed my name as Esther on my application. I tried not to fret about it. When I walked into Beau's apartment, all the boys were hanging out in the kitchen drinking beer.

"These cannolis are from Mike and Maggie's Café!" exclaimed Beau as he opened the box. "We love that place!"

"It seems wonderful. I filled out an application to work there. Maggie asked me to come in for an interview tomorrow. The only problem is that I put Esther down as my name and now I'm nervous that they will ask me for some proof of identification…"

"Just tell them you lost it!" Beau suggested. "Look, Angela, I'm sure you'll be fine! Or…should I start calling you Esther now?" Dante and Mario joined his laughter.

"Thank goodness we call you 'Mom,'" Dante chuckled. "It might get difficult to try to keep up with your aliases."

"Well, hopefully an alias will keep Aaron Stone off my tail. Hand me a cannoli—I've been dying to have one!" Mario handed over the box. I bit into the crispy fried pastry dough and the taste of the delicious, sweet, creamy filling nearly made me swoon. *Who would have ever thought that ricotta cheese and sugar could make me temporarily forget that my ex-boyfriend is trying to hunt me down?*

* * * *

Aaron climbed into his limousine and slammed the door, angrily. "Get me Michael Victory on the phone NOW!" he roared at his driver.

"Right away, sir," replied Richard, coolly. Aaron held the ringing phone to his ear.

"Hello, sir," came the low, confident voice of Michael Victory from the other end of the line.

"I am leaving the Middle East tonight. I will stop off in Nashville to make inquiries there myself, since my men are seemingly incompetent. How could they let her get away? And then I will be in New York soon. This is YOUR responsibility now, Victory, and I want her FOUND! She is in New York and you are NOT allowed to let her slip through your fingers again!"

"Yes sir. She must have some kind of help on her end that we are not aware of. We pulled the phone records of her son, Nicholas, but they are not showing any communication with her. She is proving particularly difficult to locate and she is skilled in evading your men. However, we are on her trail and will have her soon."

"Soon isn't good enough, Victory. Get her NOW. No excuses. I want her at my estate before I return to New York." He hung up before Michael Victory could even reply.

March 23, 2012
The Jewish Temple

My alarm went off. I rolled over to check my phone—I needed to make sure Nick didn't text me during the night. Knowing I only had a few hours before my interview, I climbed out of bed and headed for the shower. As I stepped under the stream of water, I had the strangest feeling that Aaron was using some sort of witchcraft to try to find me. I thought of his smile, his laugh…it was as if Aaron was reminding me that I loved him.

I have to be strong and fight these feelings I realized. *His chip that once tracked me can't harm me anymore. The only way Aaron can possibly find me now is through demons and evil spells.* I could faintly hear his voice in my mind, calling to me over and over, telling me to come home, and that he loved me. It was so difficult to fight those feelings. I fell on my knees right there in the shower and asked God to help me get Aaron's voice out of my head. I hoped He would block Aaron Stone's attempts to steal my soul. As I finished praying and stepped out of the shower, my phone beeped with a message from Nick.

'Hey, Mom, just sending you an update—no word on Denver yet. I heard that Aaron is going crazy trying to find you; he had all my phone records pulled. I haven't talked to him since the last time he came looking for you.'

'Hi, Nick. Just let me know immediately if you find anything out about Denver. Did they have the funeral for Kaitlin yet? If so, I'm sure Aaron sent his men to the funeral looking for me.'

'Yes, they had the funeral already. I went. There were several people there, Mom.' Tears welled up in my eyes at the thought.

'I wish I could have been there…'

'I know, Ma. You would have, if Aaron wasn't after you. Aaron's the reason she's gone! We will stop him, Mom. What's going on there?'

'I have an interview at nine-thirty. Wish me luck?'

'Good luck, Mom! I'll keep you posted on what's going on here. I love you.'

'Love you too, Nick.'

Oh, God, I really need this job! I need to save up enough money to get Nick out of Nashville. If for any reason I need to leave NYC, I would feel better knowing that Nick is safely with his brothers. I went downstairs, out the front door, and down the block to the cafe. On my way, I happened upon a newsstand. I glanced over to see what was on display and a headline caught my eye. It was on the front page of a popular New York paper. The headline read, 'The BEAST is Coming.' My curiosity piqued, I bought the paper so I could read the article. I had an hour to kill anyway, so I walked to the coffee shop at the end of the street. I ordered a small coffee and opened up my paper.

There he was, Aaron Stone himself, gazing at me from a large photograph of him shaking hands with the president of the European Commission. The article went on to explain that the new computer, the BEAST, would be in place by December. The world's currency would no longer be necessary and each person will be able to choose where they wanted to place their microchip tag, but doctors were still conducting tests on the RFID tags to find out where the best placement was on the human body—the hand or the head.

Right underneath that article was another entitled, 'Vatican Calling for New World Economic Order.' This article explained that the Vatican was calling for a New World Financial System to rise up and take over the world's crippled economy. The Pontiff planned to employ this order through the United Nations.

I looked down at my watch and realized that I only had twenty minutes to walk over to my interview. I downed the last bit of my coffee and folded the paper under my arm. In those twenty minutes leading up to my interview, I thought about Aaron and what he used to say to me about the world—how everyone would look to him as a savior. He would loosen the grip of the men of power who controlled the world through politics, while promising to bring peace and relief. But as it was foretold, the Antichrist would eventually bring only destruction.

Kathryn Samuel

The beep of my text notification broke into my thoughts. I reached into the pocket of my black, cotton jacket, pulled my phone out, and saw that it was a message in the game. *Nick.*

The message read: 'Hey Ma. I have some news about Aaron Stone. This morning, he was on his way to Chicago with his lawyer, Frank. They're being transported by helicopter to some kind of secret meeting about the Federal Reserve in Oak Park. It's a place called Unity Temple off of Lake Street Drive.'

I messaged him back immediately. 'Nick, how do you know this?'

'One of Aaron's new bodyguards is my old classmate. When he caught wind of the fact that Aaron was hunting you down, he contacted me. He promised he'd keep me updated on Aaron's movements. We can stay one step ahead of him.'

'Wow, that is awesome, Nick. What's his name?'

'His name is Michael Victory. He says their next stop is New York in a few days. There is another big Federal Reserve meeting there. Very high-profile leaders are supposed to show up, but it's a secret meeting.'

'Thanks for the update, Nick. Please be careful. And when you talk to Michael, tell him to be careful too. Remember…when it comes to Aaron Stone, we're not battling against flesh and blood.'

'I know, Ma. I will warn Michael. I love you. Tell my brothers and Beau I said hello and to take good care of you.'

As I approached Maggie and Mike's, I could see Maggie outside, cleaning the front door windows.

"Good morning, Esther," she greeted me. I was not yet used to being called Esther. There was a slight pause before I returned her greeting.

"Good morning, Maggie," I said softly. She didn't seem to notice any hesitation.

"Mike is inside if you want to go in ahead of me. I will be right in. Just need to finish wiping down these windows."

"Okay, see you inside," I responded, gingerly pulling the door open to keep my fingerprints off of the glass door she'd just cleaned.

A brawny looking man with dark hair was shuffling a pile of paperwork at one of the side tables when I walked in. As soon as he saw me, he stood up and held out his hand to meet me. His voice was raspy, but warm.

"Good morning, Esther. You're here for your interview?"

"Yes," I nodded, shaking his hand. "I hope I'm not keeping you from your paperwork."

"No, not at all Esther, I'm just looking for a receipt. Besides, we could really use some help around here, so you are a blessing!" There was no way he could know that I felt the same way about him and Maggie.

"Let's get you started," he continued, motioning for me to sit down. "What hours are you looking for?"

"I am very flexible at the moment. Any hours that are available are perfectly fine with me."

"Great! Well, Esther, we are looking for part-time help, Monday through Thursday, from six in the evening to eleven. Would you be interested?" I absolutely was.

"Definitely. What is the position?"

"You will basically be an assistant manager, helping Maggie up front so she can take care of more back of the house issues. She tends to drown in paperwork," he chuckled before continuing, "I think we would probably need you to bartend occasionally as well."

"That sounds perfect, Mike. When would you like me to start?"

"Tomorrow? Around five? Does that come across as being too desperate?" I laughed. If only they knew how desperate I was.

"That sounds perfect. Thank you so much!"

"Absolutely. Our dress code is pretty simple: a white shirt with black dress pants, a black belt, and black non-slip shoes." Mike reached across the table to shake my hand again.

"Welcome to the family, Esther." I smiled.

"Thank you, again, Mike." Maggie was walking in as I stood up.

Mike kissed her on the cheek and said, "I'm going to run to the bank before we open."

"Okay, see you in a little bit then." Mike grabbed his keys off of the bar, tucked his blue deposit bag under his arm, and smiled back at us as he walked out the door. Maggie turned to me, expectantly.

"Well, how did it go?"

"I got the job," I said, grinning.

"Great, so you have your schedule and you know the dress code?"

"Yes," I nodded. "Thank you."

"Wonderful. I am so glad you took the position, Esther. Now, did Mike go over what we will pay you?" I'd almost forgotten that part. I shook my head.

"No, he didn't."

"Okay, we are going to pay you twenty dollars an hour, plus whatever you make in tips. Will that work for you?"

"That's perfect. Will I be paid weekly or biweekly?"

"We pay weekly here."

"Great. Well, I will see you tomorrow, Maggie. Thanks again."

"Thank you, Esther," she responded. When she smiled, I noticed that Maggie had the most beautiful white teeth.

I headed out the door, reminding myself not to touch the clean glass, and began to walk in the direction of the nearest department store. I needed to buy a few white shirts before my first day of work.

Lost in my own thoughts, I was in the men's department when I noticed someone walked very closely behind me. That same, familiar stench of sulfur filled the air and my stomach twisted into knots. A shiver ran down my spine and I began to walk faster. The evil that radiated behind me felt stronger than any other that I had encountered recently. If I could feel his presence, I wondered if he could feel mine. All I knew for sure was that I couldn't turn around. The last thing I needed was some demon to recognize me when Aaron Stone was on his way to New York City. I began to pray, asking God to show me what to do.

Out of nowhere, a little boy came running past me. A woman ahead of me began to yell with a thick Spanish accent, "Matthew! Matthew, come back here!" All of a sudden, I heard some kind of commotion going on behind me, and the sound of bags dropping on the floor. I stole a quick glance over my shoulder to see a blond-haired man trying to gather the contents of his scattered bags.

I caught his eyes while he was looking toward the boy. There were a deep, glowing red behind his black-framed glasses. His countenance was beastly. My heart feared for the little boy. A large, Spanish woman with long, dark curly hair came running over to the boy and grabbed his hand.

"I'm so sorry, sir," she said apologetically to the blonde-haired man. She began to speak rapidly in Spanish to the boy as she dragged him away. While watching them leave temporarily distracted the man, I disappeared into a crowd of chattering women.

As soon as I was out of his sight, I turned into a different aisle, hiding behind a rack of floral-patterned sundresses. My heart was pounding as I peeked through the rack to see him pass by the group of women. Peace washed over me again. I knew I was safe again. *For now.* I wiped a small bead of sweat from my forehead and turned around. Directly behind me, there was a rack of white, button-down shirts. I laughed to myself. Not only had God protected me, but He also brought me right where I needed to be. *That was a close one. How am I ever going to work in a public place without these demons finding me?* I wondered. *I have to find a way to keep them from entering Mike & Maggie's cafe.*

I grabbed a few white shirts that appeared to be my size and headed for the checkout line. As soon as I had paid for them, I slipped out of the store and headed for Beau's place. "Anybody home?" I sang as I opened the door to his loft. There was no answer, so I assumed the boys were all at work. I walked into my bedroom any hung my new white shirts up in my closet. Returning to the living room, I plopped down on the couch and turned on the television. I laid my head back, closing my eyes just for a moment...

The next thing I knew, I was walking down a busy road. Looking up ahead in the distance, I could see a considerably large, exquisite building sitting on top of a hill. As I approached it, I noticed that it resembled the Jewish Temple that Solomon built for the Hebrew people in biblical times.

A great, stone wall led to a beautiful portico at the front of the Temple. I glanced around for any sign of danger before I entered the portico. The inside was made of pure gold. The walls were paneled in pine and covered with gold trim. It was adorned with palm trees and carved cherubim. As I looked around, I noticed that I was not alone. People who appeared to be Hebrew began to enter the portico. I noticed a group in a circle, standing just off to the right of me.

I overheard them saying to each other that they had moved from Israel to be close to Aaron Stone. They called him *Prince Aaron Stone*. I wandered away from them, toward an inner room. Glancing inside, I saw him. Aaron Stone sat on a golden throne, dressed in a flowing red, blue, and purple robe tied with a golden sash. On his head rested a solid gold crown. People bowed down before him, worshipping him.

He saw me. Those eyes, glowing a bright blue, were just like the first time we'd met, but this time, a flash came from his eyes, as though he was pointing a bright laser directly into my eyes. I felt the light penetrating my body. I tried to take a step back, thinking I could run. But I was completely helpless, as if his light had paralyzed me. All I could do was fall to my knees.

With the slam of his fist, he yelled at me, "GET UP, ANGELA!" His voice was stern; his stare was glassy. "Why did you leave me?" Aaron demanded. "You *know* who I am. You *know* what I am capable of." My entire body trembled in fear. The man I once loved had now become my worst enemy. He was far more powerful than I would ever be. He stood up from his throne and began to walk toward me. Each step seemed to echo in the great hall and chills ran down my spine. "Look at me, Angela!" He was so close I could almost feel his warm breath, but I refused to look up. Taking a handful of my hair, he pulled my head back. "I SAID, LOOK AT ME!"

I whimpered, unwilling to meet his eyes. "Please, Aaron. Don't hurt me." He tightened his grip on my hair as he wrapped it around his hand. With the other hand, he grabbed my neck and began to squeeze. I could barely breathe.

He leaned over and whispered in my ear, "You are mine, Angela, and you will pay for walking away from me." Aaron began to softly kiss my jawline. "Look at me, Angela," he said, more gently than before. I couldn't look into his eyes. He could take control of me if I looked into his eyes.

"No," I refused.

"You *will*," he growled, tilting my head back even further. I thought he would snap my neck until I heard...

"Mom, Mom! Wake up! You're having a dream! Stop crying!" I jumped off of the couch, my heart pounding like a race horse. *It was just a dream*, I reassured myself. I was cold, shaking from the sweat that drenched my body. *Oh, my God*, it felt so real to me. Mario put his hand on my shoulder. "Mom, calm down. You're okay. It was only a dream."

I looked at him and mumbled, "Thank God." But inside, I wondered...*Was that a dream? Or a vision of things to come?*

March 24, 2012
Maggie & Mike's Café

I woke to a notification a little after five the next morning. It was a message from Nick. I opened the game and clicked on our private chat. 'Ma? You awake?'

'Yes, Nick, I'm here. Is everything okay?'

'Yeah, Ma, Michael Victory sent me a message today. He is headed to New York City with Aaron Stone for three weeks. They'll be staying at the "W" instead of where Aaron usually stays.'

'That's strange. Why the change of plans?'

'Not sure, just giving you a heads up.'

'Thanks, honey. How are you doing? Any word on Denver yet?'

'They think she might have burned in the fire, but they still haven't found any conclusive evidence.'

I felt a knot in my stomach and I feared the worst. Denver and I had become such close friends. While my house was on the market, we went out to dinner several times together. When she went through her divorce, I made sure I was there for her. She had always seemed concerned about my relationship with Aaron, but was very supportive of me making my own decisions. Denver was a true friend who loved me for who I was, not for what I did.

I thought about Kaitlin and how much I missed her. I remember the three of us, Kaitlin, Denver, and myself, laughing in a restaurant about the craziest shit that always seemed to happen to us. But now, Kaitlin was dead and Denver was missing. Who would have ever thought that the charming man who had coming into the restaurant would have turned out to be the Antichrist?

'Ma, are you still there?'

'Yes, Nick, I am. Sorry, I was just reminiscing about Denver and I can't believe she's still missing.'

'Okay, just making sure you're all right. I am going to go back to bed. Tell everyone I said hello.'

'Will do, honey. I love you, Nick. Stay safe and thank you for the update.'

'Anytime, Ma. Love you, too. Talk to you soon.'

I glanced at my clock. It was quarter to six, so I rolled over and tried to go back to sleep. For close to an hour, I couldn't seem to turn my mind off, but eventually the coolness of my pillow and the warm of the comforter had me drifting off. When I woke up a few hours later, I realized that no one was home. I looked around the kitchen and decided to surprise the boys by baking them some brownies.

While the brownies were in the oven, I heard a knock at the door. I stopped what I was doing and began to walk toward the door, but suddenly, something inside said, *"Don't!"* I quietly peered through the peephole. On the other side of the door stood a man dressed in black. A long scar ran down the side of his cheek. His eyes were beginning to turn read. *Holy cow! What the hell am I going to do?* All I knew was that I was not going to open the door! I silently checked the chain on the door and tiptoed back into the kitchen, praying the man would go away. I heard him knock a few more times and then it was quiet again. I waited several agonizingly long seconds, then tiptoed back over to the peephole. Sure enough, the man in black was gone.

I thanked God, but wondered who the man was and why he had come. If he was a friend of Beau's, that would prove to be a problem. If he came while I was there, my cover would be blown.

Walking back into the kitchen, I waited for the brownies to finish baking. Once they were cooled, I arranged them on a silver tray I found in the cabinet and put them on the table with a note that said, "Enjoy boys, I love you." Guilt washed over me. If I wanted to protect my boys, it was time for me to move somewhere secluded. As soon as I could save enough money to do so, I would leave. I thought of Mike and Maggie, hoping that I wasn't endangering them by working in their café.

Later that afternoon, when I was getting ready for work, I felt anxious. I knew by the end of the night I would be fine, but the image of the man in black with the red eyes was burned into my mind.

What I wouldn't give to have my old life back! My friends, my family, my job…before Aaron Stone came along, everything had been pretty damn near perfect. I wished I could wake up from the never-ending nightmare that had become my life.

I grabbed my purse and flung it over my shoulder, taking a cautious look through the peephole before I walked out. Once I was in the hallway, I looked both ways, just to be certain no one was waiting for me. As soon as I got to Maggie & Mike Café, I had to bypass a long line of people already waiting outside for a table. Once inside, I could hear Mike's voice, slightly muffled over the loudness of the crowd.

"Hey, Esther, go on back to the office. I will meet you there in a minute. I need to get your time card. Chase will be training you tonight." Maggie glanced over her shoulder to smile at me while she was pouring a draft beer. Every barstool in the café was occupied by a man or a woman in business casual dress—they had obviously just gotten off of work. As I turned back around, I noticed a tall, extremely good-looking, dark-haired guy with the most amazing big brown eyes walking toward me.

He held out his hand for me to shake, "Hi, Esther. I'm Chase. I'll be training you tonight." I couldn't seem to remember any words for a second. I was completely tongue-tied.

"Is something wrong?" he asked.

"No, not at all. I'm sorry; you just caught me off guard," I finally responded.

"Well, if you're ready, it's really busy; we need to get out there."

I looked at those mesmerizing, big, brown eyes and said, "Okay, let's go. I'm ready."

We pushed our way through the crowd and behind the bar. The people seemed to just keep coming. I followed Chase around, asking questions and observing his actions. When the crowd finally began to die down a few hours later, I took a deep breath.

"Wow, who would have ever thought that this place could get so packed?" I remarked.

"Yeah," Chase agreed. "This is the hangout for the locals after work." I studied Chase for a moment and realized that he had distracted me all night from the thought of demons and my dead friends. And Aaron Stone.

April 15, 2012
Hard to Say Goodbye

When I woke up, I could *feel* him. I knew that he was in New York City. There was an overwhelming tension in my chest. I was sure that he could feel me, too. As much as I had tried to break the ties I felt to him, I couldn't seem to do it. It was as if I could hear him audibly saying, "I will find you, Angela. You belong to me. I am getting closer. Come back to me before you feel my wrath. If you come back, I will forgive you for leaving me."

"*Stop* it!" I said aloud, covering my ears with my hands, as though that would block his voice. *Angela*, a voice in the room gently beckoned to me. *You are in control. It's up to you to listen or not.* "I wish it would be that simple," I snapped back. *You have a freewill, Angela. Use it.* I began to meditate on that precious gift that was given to me. I could choose to ignore Aaron's voice in my head. No matter what he did to my body, he would never take my soul. He could call me *his*, but I was still a child of God's. "Thank you for protecting me," I said, acknowledging His presence there with me in my bedroom. Peace washed over me and I felt the tension in my

155

body subsiding. Now, all I had to do was keep my eyes peeled. Aaron Stone was in New York City for the next three weeks.

* * * *

Weeks later, things began to calm down. Chase and I started dating. I couldn't help myself; I knew being with Chase was dangerous. If Aaron Stone ever found out, he would kill us both. I had decided it was time to move out of NYC. I just wasn't sure how to tell Chase. After our shift one extremely busy Friday night, Chase and I decided to walk down to this small jazz club at the end of the block. It was a great place to unwind after a stressful night, with a glass of wine and some soft jazz music. I decided it was the right time to tell him about my decision to move away.

We took a late stroll, hand-in-hand, and I noticed the full moon shining brightly above us. It was too perfect; I didn't want to ruin it. Suddenly, Chase stopped and wrapped his arms around me. He leaned forward and gave me a long, passionate kiss. It was almost as if he *knew* that I was leaving. I looked up into those big, brown eyes I adored, and I could see that he was trying not to cry. When he looked down into my eyes, I saw the moonlight reflecting off of his tears. Feeling his strong arms around me gave me a sense of security. For that brief moment, even in the sadness, I felt such a peace. I never wanted to leave his arms. If I could have captured that moment and saved it, I would still be living in it.

All of a sudden, I heard a gun's loud bang. A warm, sticky substance began to cover my hands and the heaviness of Chase's body collapsed in my arms. When I pulled back, Chase fell to the ground. He was bleeding from a bullet wound in his back. I started screaming.

Two men dressed completely in black jumped out of a black SUV. As they ran toward me, I started yelling at them, "Please, *please* can you help me? Please hurry! Someone shot my boyfriend!" As they approached Chase, one bent over his bleeding, limp body and put his hand into his back jean pocket. He pulled out Chase's wallet. As he began looking through it, I yelled, "What are you *doing*? Why are you not helping him?"

The man slipped Chase's wallet into his coat pocket and looked up to smile at me. His eyes were glowing red. The other man stepped over Chase's body and grabbed my arm, twisting it as he dragged me back toward their black SUV. I started kicking and screaming as loud as I could. His deep, raspy voice sounded strangely calm as he said, "If you kick me one more time, I will kill you right here." Those glowing, red eyes didn't even blink as he shoved me into the backseat.

If there had been any doubt in my mind that Aaron Stone was behind all of this, it was gone in that instant. I shivered, completely overtaken by fear. Flashes of my children raced through my mind. *How did this happen?* I asked myself. *Was I so intrigued by Chase that I let my guard down? Did I neglect the gift that was supposed to protect me?* I needed to calm down and think quickly; I was in a life or death situation. I knew I had to hide my cell phone somehow. If they found it, they would take it, and I would have no way to communicate with Nick. And, if they could figure out a way to get to my messages on the game, they would find out that Michael Victory had been informing us about Aaron Stone's movements. They would most likely kill Michael Victory for betraying Aaron. *Oh, God! Where* are *You?* I cried out in my mind as I sat in the backseat.

The man seated next to me, the one who had shoved me into the SUV, was wearing a hat with a skull and cross bones symbol on it. Aaron had an almost identical hat. The other man, the one who had taken Chase's wallet, was driving. They both reeked of sulfur. Between the erratic driving and the sulfur smell, I was getting sick to my stomach. I covered my mouth and began dry heaving. The man next to me noticed. "I'm going to be sick," I said, weakly.

"Hey, pull over," he yelled at the driver. "She's going to throw up!" The driver swerved over to the side of the road, threw the SUV into park, and jumped out to open my door.

"If you try any funny business…" He didn't finish his sentence. In fact, he barely got out of the way in time. I projectile vomited all over the side of the road.

They exchanged disgusted looks. The man who'd been next to me jumped out and walked around to the back of the SUV with the driver. I continued to vomit as I leaned out the door and I could hear them talking. They were far enough away that I knew they couldn't see me. It was the perfect chance to hide my cell phone.

Exaggerating the sound of me getting sick, I reached into my pocket and made sure the phone was on silent. I managed to find a hole in the carpet just under the driver's seat, so I slid the phone in, praying they were not watching me from behind. As soon as I was done, I leaned back out of the SUV, made a dry heaving noise, and then sat back down in my seat. The driver was the first one back into the SUV. Slamming the door behind him, he tilted the rearview mirror down to look at me. "I will *not* stop again, Angela," he said.

As my eyes met his in the mirror, I noticed something strange. His eyes weren't glowing at all. *Could he be Michael Victory?* I wondered to myself.

"I'm fine now," I replied honestly. "You won't have to stop again." The other man climbed back into the SUV and we were off again. My mind wandered off as the SUV sped down winding back roads for what felt like hours. I could almost see Chase's face again and feel the warmth of his blood on my fingertips. What if they planned to go after my boys next? Fear for the safety of my children told me to be obedient to whatever their demands were.

Underneath us, the tires began to hesitate as we crossed an enormous bridge. Although the bridge was dimly lit, I could see a river below us. When we finally crossed the bridge, we passed a sign that said, '*Welcome to Sleepy Hollow.*'

There was something unnerving about the name of the town and the way the mountains glowed in the distance with light from scattered mansions. We turned into a long driveway lined with soft white light that illuminated the pavement winding up to the security entrance beside the iron gates. The SUV slowed and a security guard approached the driver's side window.

I couldn't hear what he said to the driver, but I noticed him leaning in the window to look at me. He nodded his head, smiled smugly, and waved us on. A moment later, the gates opened and we continued up the driveway toward one of the lit mansions high up on the mountainside.

As we approached the circular driveway in front of the mansion, an older woman in a black and white maid's uniform stepped out of the two solid oak front doors with a phone in her right hand. "It's the boss," she said in a thick Russian accent, handing the phone through the driver's window as he parked the SUV. "He asked to speak with you."

"Guten tag," he replied, accepting the phone.

While the man who was seated next to me opened the side door and climbed out, I leaned forward, straining to try to hear the voice on the other end of the line. I wondered if it was Aaron Stone.

"Ja, ja," the driver responded to the voice on the other end of the line, "auf-Wiedersehen." He handed the phone back to the maid and his door squealed as it opened. He walked over to my door, opened it, and looked straight into my eyes.

"Please do not struggle with me, Angela. It will only make this more difficult for you," he instructed, extending his hand to me so I could climb out of my seat. I accepted his hand and stepped out of the SUV.

The scene before me was overwhelming. Dark and unfamiliar, the shadows of the mansion's surroundings appeared far more ominous than they would in daylight. As we entered the spacious foyer, I noticed that the decor was European-style. The white, marble floors cast an ancient, Roman ambiance. In the center of the room, a circular cherry wood table sat above a black and white Persian rug. The sweet aroma of freshly cut flowers filled the air. The flowers were displayed in a crystal vase on top of the table. An exquisite chandelier sparkled like diamonds overhead. Off to the right stood a grand, white, marble staircase with Jackson Pollock paintings lining the walls. The staircase wrapped up toward the ceiling. Black, wrought iron rails lined the steps in stark contrast. I heard the echo of voices coming from above.

A German accent came from behind me, "Are you hungry or thirsty, Angela?" I turned to see that the men had disappeared and another woman in a maid's uniform stood behind me. This time, a blonde in her late forties.

"Angela, my name is Bethany," she seemed to read my mind. "I will be your personal maid while you are at the Mansion. Can I bring you anything before we get you settled?" I stared into her green eyes for a moment. She was speaking to me as though I was a guest, not a prisoner. If she knew my name, I wondered what else she knew about me. It was time for me to get some answers.

"Actually, could you tell me where I am, Bethany?" Her face spelled disappointment.

"Angela, I am sorry, but I am not authorized to divulge that information." A strong hand gripped my arm, whipping me around.

"Ouch!" I yelped. "You're hurting me!" Using his other hand, he pulled my other arm back and restrained me from moving. I fought back, trying to break free, but his grip was too strong.

As if in slow motion, I saw her coming toward me in a deep purple gown. Her thick, curly hair bounced with each step she took. Perfect posture held her slender shoulders back as she flicked the needle she held. Her exotic features seemed to soften as she spoke to me. "Angela, you have had a stressful night. You need to relax."

I looked straight into her brown eyes and said, "No, thank you." She laughed, a sinister laugh, and shook her head.

"Neither of us has a choice, Angela. I am just following orders. And so will you." To no avail, I struggled harder to break free, but another set of hands arrived to restrain me. Within seconds, the needle was in my arm, its contents surging through my blood stream. Everything became blurry and I felt my body become limp. It was all I could do to stand on my own feet. The voices around me began to fade in and out.

"Angela," the woman in purple with the brown eyes and curly hair was inches from my face, "Angela, relax. Just relax." It all faded to black.

May 2, 2012
The Plush Room

I awoke with cottonmouth and a severe headache. My eyes searched for something to drink, but even if they found it, I couldn't have reached out. There were restraints around my wrists and ankles. I could hear a metal clank as I pushed back the golden, charmeuse satin comforter with my knees and pulled myself up against the bed frame.

There was no telling how long I had been out or where I was. I assumed from the decor of the room that I was still in the mansion. The walls held paintings of Greek mythology. Sheer, white curtains flowed from white columns surrounding the bed I was on. Directly overhead, a gaudy looking, bronze celestial medallion was suspended from the ceiling.

I soon found myself nodding in and out of consciousness, still fighting the effects of the sedative. A familiar voice floated toward me. The smell of his Black Classic cologne filled the air. I opened my eyes, searching for his face. But I felt him before I saw him. His hand gently caressed my cheek. The smoothness of his freshly shaved face brushed against mine.

All I wanted to do in that moment was put my arms around Aaron Stone and kiss him passionately. I missed the sound of his voice, the way he held me, the scent of his body lingering on mine. But I was terrified of what he was going to do to me.

"Angela," he whispered into my ear. "I've missed you, darling. I am going to take good care of you now. I won't ever let you out of my sight again." Aaron wrapped his arms around me and pulled me closer to him so he could press his lips against mine. When he pulled back, I looked up into his eyes.

"Aaron, please untie me. I want to hold you."

Immediately, he stretched across my body to loosen the straps on my wrists. As soon as my left hand was free, I slipped it around his neck. Shutting my eyes tightly, taking in deep breaths of his aroma, and feeling the weight of his frame against mine, I almost forgot everything. I almost forgot about Chase's dead body on the sidewalk. I almost forgot about my fear for my boys and why I had escaped to NYC. When I opened my eyes again, I realized I was alone and still bound to the bed. It was only a dream. Tears began to run down my face as I wept softly.

"Chase," I cried out, sputtering my tears. "They left him lying there in the middle of the sidewalk, bleeding to death! Please God! Let him live. And my children! They're probably worried sick about me..." Whether it was the sedative or the weakness in my body from lack of sustenance, I felt myself fading again. *God,* I prayed silently, *please let Michael Victory tell Nick where I am.*

* * * *

"Angela? Angela, did you make the coffee yet?" Kyle's voice floated down the hall. As I rubbed my eyes, I looked up to see Kyle's face staring back at mine. He looked down at his watch, slightly annoyed.

"Angela, it's already seven. You promised you'd make me coffee. I have to be at my meeting by eight-thirty." I sat up, yawning and rubbed my eyes again. Sure enough, I was in our old home. It was the same sofa, the same family pictures, and the same big screen television. It was as if Kyle had never left.

"Oh my God, Kyle! Is this a dream?"

"Angela, this is not a dream! You said you were coming in to make me coffee, but now I find you here on the sofa with the television on, sound asleep!" I heard a soft whining and when I looked at the floor, I saw my little puppy that had run away shortly after the divorce. I wasn't dreaming! The nightmare was finally over!

Jumping up off of the couch, I put my arms around Kyle and gave him a big kiss. He took a step back and stared at me with bewilderment. "What was that for, Angela? What is going on?"

"Oh, Kyle, I had the most terrible dream you could ever imagine! You left me for a younger woman and I met a man at the restaurant who claimed to be the Anti-Christ, Lucifer incarnate! I ended up falling in love with him and he microchipped me so he could control me. He kept talking about the New World Order he would put into place and how he was from some alien race..."

Kyle interrupted me with a smirk. "Well, Dorothy, you're home now and Toto is right beside you." Laughing at his own joke, he walked into the kitchen to make his coffee.

"It's not funny, Kyle!" I continued, following him into the kitchen. "It was *real*. At least, it was real to me. Come on, let me tell you the rest!"

"Okay, tell me while you're making coffee, Angela." I looked at him and smiled. "You know, Kyle, I love you. I am so happy to be home."

"'There's no place like home,'" he quoted, continuing with his joke as I rolled my eyes. "Go ahead and finish your dream, Angela."

"Now, as soon as I found out that this guy, Aaron Stone, was leaving for the Middle East, I quickly called Denver—"

"Who's Denver?" Kyle looked confused. *Oh yeah*, I realized, *she's still alive, but I don't actually know her.*

"Denver was our real estate agent. She helped me sell this house after you left." It was Kyle's turn to roll his eyes.

"Right, I forgot; I left you for a younger woman..."

"Come on, Kyle, just let me finish."

"Go ahead."

"Well, Denver introduced me to her boyfriend, a man named Dr. Evans, who deactivated my microchip. But once Aaron Stone found out, he had everyone killed!" Kyle looked surprised.

"Wow, this Aaron Stone doesn't play around."

"He was in love with me, Kyle!"

"Alright, Angela, are you almost finished?" There was a hint of jealousy in Kyle's voice as he reached for a coffee cup from the cabinet. "I have to go soon."

"Okay, so when I found out that everyone in Dr. Evans's office had died, I found out that Aaron had also killed my friend Kaitlin and bombed Denver's house. So, I packed up and went to hide in NYC with Dante and Mario at Beau's loft."

"Now, that's funny," Kyle said, pouring his coffee.

I continued, ignoring his interruption.

"I found a job in NYC at a café called Maggie and Mike's, where I met a guy named Chase, who was a server. We went on a couple of dates, but Aaron Stone found out and sent his men to kill Chase. After they killed Chase, they kidnapped me and brought me to a mansion in Sleepy Hollow where a woman drugged me and tied me to a bed for days. And then I woke up here!"

Kyle nodded, processing what I had said. "That does sound like a scary dream, Angela. What did the Anti-Christ want with you?"

"I was never really sure myself, but I assumed it had to do with my beliefs."

"Well, thank God you're home now, Angela. Home safe and sound with your 'Prince Charming' who is dying for another cup of coffee," he hinted, handing me his empty mug. I smiled as I poured, but something still disturbed me. The dream had felt so real.

June 2, 2013
There is No Place like Home

It was so nice to be at home again, safe and sound. I didn't take Kyle for granted; I had missed the way it felt to be wrapped in his arms. I quickly returned to my normal daily routine, but the dream I'd had continued to haunt me. Conversations about aliens, religion, and politics made me skittish, bringing flashbacks of Aaron. The worst part was that I was afraid to fall asleep at night, certain I'd wake up still tied to that bed.

Days passed, dark circles appeared under my eyes, and I began to experience severe headaches from my insomnia. On top of that, I was constantly paranoid. I had panic attacks every time I left our house. My fear was that Aaron would send his men to kill Kyle and kidnap me. When I saw Nick, I repeatedly asked him if he had gone to school with a guy named Michael Victory.

"No, Ma, that was just a dream," Nick would say. Kyle became very concerned.

"Angela, you need to sleep. Maybe you should go see a psychiatrist about your insomnia." I acted like I agreed, but something told me to stay away from doctors. I couldn't risk Aaron Stone finding out that I had told his secrets to someone. Doing so would endanger my children, my husband, and myself. My life became a living hell. And the worst part was that I began to believe that it was a hell created by my own mind.

Aaron Stone was a fictitious character created by my subconscious, but there were moments when I found myself missing his charisma and his arrogance. I wondered if he knew where I was; I wondered if he had somehow managed to continue to control my mind. One morning, as those thoughts swam in my head, Kyle began to stir beside me. His alarm had not yet gone off, but he sat up in bed.

"Good morning, honey," I said, leaning over to kiss his cheek.

"Good morning," he replied in a raspy voice. "Did you sleep at all?"

"No," I answered honestly. "I think I am going to call a doctor today. These headaches are unbearable." Kyle yawned and nodded.

"That's a great idea. Why don't you call this morning so they can get you in sometime this week?" I pushed the comforter off of me and put my feet on the floor. As I reached for the house phone, I had a flashback. I was in the SUV again, fear coursing through my veins, as I searched frantically for a place to hide my cell phone. I'd hidden it in a hole in the carpet under the driver's seat...

"Honey, have you seen my cell phone?" I turned to ask. Kyle frowned and shook his head.

"No, I haven't. Did you lose it?"

"I'm not sure," I admitted. I hadn't seen it in days. It occurred to me that aside from talking to Kaitlin and Denver, I had rarely used my cell phone. I rubbed my temples, wishing I could rub away the splitting headache.

"Don't worry, sweetheart," Kyle said, kissing my shoulder. "If you don't find it, we'll get you another one."

"It's just odd that it could disappear without me noticing it," I replied. I walked into the living room and typed 'psychiatrist' into the computer's homepage search engine. Several doctors in the area popped up. The one that caught my eye had four stars next to it, *Dr. Jason Samuel, M.D., Franklin, TN.*

Using the house phone, I dialed the number. A sweet sounding receptionist answered on the second ring. "Dr. Samuel's office. How may I help you?"

"Hi, my name is Angela Russo and I was hoping to make an appointment."

"Certainly. Are you a current patient of Dr. Samuel?"

"No, I'm not."

"Okay, well, it looks like our first available appointment will be next Friday at ten forty-five." *Another week of these headaches…*

"Great. I'll take it."

"Alright, Angela Russo, I will put you down for that appointment. Would you mind coming in about ten to fifteen minutes early to fill out some paperwork?"

"Sure, I will be there next Friday at ten thirty."

"Perfect. We'll see you then. Take care." *I'll try*, I thought as I hung up. When I went back to the bedroom, Kyle had just finished showering. I told him about the appointment.

"Angela, that's great. I will make sure I have that morning off so I can take you." He wrapped his arms around me and I breathed in his scent.

"Thank you, Kyle. I love you so much."

"I love you, too," he said, letting me go so he could finish getting dressed.

Later that morning, after Kyle had left for work, I pulled my journal out of my nightstand in the bedroom, hoping that if I took the time to write it down, I could make some sense of my crazy dream. As I flipped through the journal, searching for a fresh page, I noticed that there was a discrepancy in the dates. Upon more careful inspection, I realized that some of the pages were missing. Tracing my finger over one of the torn pages, I tried to recall if I had ever removed a journal entry. I continued to flip through until I found the first blank page. Oddly, the page before it was missing. With one hand holding my place, I flipped back to the last recorded date and did the math in my head. *I can't account for the last thirteen months of my life.*

My mind began to race for an explanation. *What if Aaron...?* *That was a dream, Angela. Don't lose your mind.* I tried to calm my pounding heart, but something on the blank page caught my eye. It looked like a tearstain. As I looked closer, I could make out indentations my pen had made while forming the words on the previous page.

With the journal in my hand, I hurried down the hall to our kitchen, where we kept mechanical pencils in a drawer. Sliding a piece of lead out of one of the pencils, I used a trick I'd learned in school to decipher my writing. Lightly rubbing the lead over the seemingly blank page, the date and the first line of the missing journal entry became clear:

August 12, 2012 - I think Kyle might be having an affair.

June 6, 2013
Déjà Vu

The week had crawled by. I felt I could no longer trust what appeared to be reality. I stopped talking to Kyle about my fears and kept to myself.

That Friday morning, I woke up to rain pounding against the windowsill. I glanced at the clock. Somehow I had managed to sleep almost three hours. Kyle was gone, but he'd left a note on his pillow: *You were sleeping so soundly, Sweetheart; didn't want to wake you. Gone to get breakfast.*

His sweet note would have melted my heart if I hadn't seen those words in my journal, the ones that were seared into my mind. Just as I finished showering, I heard the front door slam.

"Kyle?" I called. "Is that you?"

"Yes," came his reply, followed by a chuckle. "It's me, your Prince Charming."

I rolled my eyes at my slowly reappearing reflection. "Aw, well, give me a minute, Prince Charming, and I'll be right out." Wrapping my bathrobe tightly around my shivering body, I opened the bathroom door. The cool air hit me immediately. I got dressed as quickly as I could. My clothes were fitting much looser than I could remember. The lack of sleep was taking its toll on my body. As I applied concealer under my eyes, my mind wandered off to the day I had gone to see Dr. Evans. My blood pressure began to rise. *Angela, snap out of it!* My mind scolded me. *That was a dream. There* is *no Dr. Evans.*

A few minutes later, I was dressed and ready to go. Emerging from the bedroom, I found Kyle on the couch, watching the news. He stood up to give me a kiss. "You look beautiful, Angela. I put your coffee and muffin on the table for you. I'm just going to take a quick shower and I'll be ready to take you."

"Okay. Thank you, Kyle. That was very sweet." Kyle pulled me close to hug me.

"Don't worry about today. It's going to be okay." I patted him on the back, feeling tears welling up in my eyes. I wished I could trust him.

"I know," I managed, choking back the tears. While Kyle showered and got ready, I ate breakfast and flipped through the channels. I couldn't watch the news anymore. It reminded me of seeing the explosions at Dr. Evans's, Kaitlin's, and Denver's.

As soon as Kyle was ready, I grabbed my purse and an umbrella. His BMW beeped as he unlocked it and the familiar sound was strangely comforting. When he'd left me, in that dream, it was one of the little things I'd missed: the sounds his car made, the way he smoothly shifted gears, the softness of his hand beneath mine, the scent of the leather interior. I couldn't catch a tear in time before it slid down my cheek. I took a deep breath and concentrated on what was in front of us.

Traffic was backed up on the highway because of the rain. We'd left with plenty of time to spare, but we were barely on time when we pulled into the parking lot. My stomach turned as I realized I was about to face emotions and fears I had been trying to avoid. I knew I'd have to explain the horrifying dream to a complete stranger. The sun was beginning to come out and the rain finally stopped. I left the umbrella in the car and followed Kyle to the directory in front of the building. "Dr. Samuel, room three-oh-one," Kyle read aloud. "We need to go to the third floor."

We entered the lobby and Kyle punched the button with the up arrow on it. As soon as the door opened, an older woman stepped out. She pulled her umbrella from underneath her arm and smiled at us. Returning her smile, I said cheerfully, "I don't think you'll be needing that; it stopped raining."

"Ah, so it has," she observed, tucking the umbrella back under her arm as she headed out the front door. "Thank you."

We got into the elevator and Kyle hit the number three button. The door shut and I could feel the jolt as the elevator ascended. It dinged at the second floor and at the third, stopping with another jolt. The door dinged open and I followed Kyle out into the hallway. We scanned the signs, looking for three hundred and one. Once we found it, Kyle opened the door for me.

The small waiting room was nearly full. I assumed that most were waiting on friends or family to come out of their session, flipping through magazines and books as they waited. I approached the receptionist. "Hi, I'm Angela Russo. I have an appointment with Dr. Samuel." The receptionist smiled warmly as she handed me a clipboard.

"Thank you for coming in early, Angela. Would you please fill this out and bring it back to me when you're done?"

"Sure," I said, accepting the clipboard. A sweet woman in her fifties moved over to an empty seat so Kyle and I could sit together as I filled out the paperwork. It was all routine, mostly information about insurance, but the question about previous hospitalization made me nervous. *They're going to think I'm insane*, I worried. I was sure to be locked up in an institution by the time my appointment was over.

When I handed the clipboard back to the receptionist, I couldn't help but notice her appearance, which I had ignored before. She had a dark complexion, with chunky highlights in her hair. Her eyes were a pretty shade of green and when she smiled again, I noticed that she had braces, which gave her a childlike appearance, although I guessed her to be in her thirties. Kyle and I waited several minutes before a nurse came out.

"Angela?" It was déjà vu. I flashed back to when Denver and I were in Dr. Evans's office.

"That's us," Kyle answered for me.

"Please follow me, Angela," the nurse said, smiling. I took one more look at Kyle. He gave me a quick hug and a wink. I obediently followed the nurse down the hallway, just as I had walked to Dr. Evans's exam room. *That was a dream, Angela. This is reality. Get a grip.*

"Dr. Samuel will be with you in just a few minutes, Angela," she reassured me and motioned for me to sit in one of the leather chairs. Once she left, I looked around the room. There were prestigious diplomas on the wall and a large bookshelf full of miscellaneous books, all shapes, colors, and sizes. A few titles caught my eye: *Recovering Our Humanity, IN-sight, It's Okay to Cry.* I shivered.

There was a knock at the door, and although it was timid, it still startled me. A man who was at least 6'3" with salt-and-pepper hair and soft, brown eyes entered the room.

"Hello, Angela, I'm Dr. Samuel." I reached out my hand to shake his.

"It's nice to meet you," I said, sincerely. I needed to make sure that I came off as sane as possible so he wouldn't think I was crazy. Once he'd gotten settled into the opposite leather chair, he looked up from the yellow notepad in his lap.

"So, Angela, what brings you into my office today?" *He's getting right to the point*, I realized with dismay. *Here goes nothing...*

"Well, it's kind of strange. I had a frightening nightmare a few weeks ago and I can't seem to sleep because of it. Now, I'm getting terrible headaches from insomnia and to be perfectly honest, I feel like it is affecting me psychologically. I have flashbacks from the dream and find myself feeling paranoid frequently."

Dr. Samuel scribbled a few notes before he responded. I wished with all of my heart that I could see what he had written. I needed some kind of warning if he thought I was crazy…

"Well, Angela, I reviewed the information you gave us and since you do not have any history of mental illness, I'm concerned that your insomnia and paranoia could be the result of a physical issue. What I'm going to do is order an MRI, so we can make sure that nothing is out of order. And, once we see the results, we can move forward from there. How does that sound?"

I was mostly relieved that he suggested the problem was with my body, not my mind.

"How long will it take to get the results?"

"Well, if I can get you in there today, I could give you your results as early as two days from now."

"That would be perfect. Thank you so much." I took a deep breath.

"Absolutely. For now, I am going to prescribe you some Xanax. It will help you relax and get some sleep for the next couple of nights until we can get you those test results."

He lifted his prescription pad out of his left breast pocket and began scribbling again. When he'd finished, he handed me the prescription and gave me instructions on how to find the radiologist's office on the first floor of the same building.

"We will call down and let them know you are on your way."
I followed him down the hall and waited while he gave instructions
to the nurse. "I'll see you in a couple of days, Angela," he said with
a friendly smile, and walked down the hall.

"Thanks again," I replied, waiting while the nurse made the
phone call.

"You're all set. As soon as we get your results, we will call
to set up your next appointment," the nurse said.

"Great," I replied and made my way back out to where Kyle
was still waiting patiently. I filled Kyle in as we took the elevator
back down to the first floor. As soon as we entered the waiting area
of radiology, which was empty, the receptionist looked up.

"Angela?"

"Yes."

"We're expecting you. Dr. Samuel's office called just a few
minutes ago. Are you ready to come on back?"

"Yes, of course."

I turned to give Kyle a kiss. "Thanks for waiting for me,
honey."

"You bet," he said with a smile. The nurse led me into a back
room to change.

"Here is your gown. It ties in the back. Be sure to remove all
of your clothing. You may leave your underwear on underneath the
gown. Once you're done, please meet me out here and I will take
you to the technician."

As soon as I was finished undressing, I slipped the gown on and tied the back. I hated everything about what I was going through. I felt like a crazy person, I didn't trust my husband, and I had splitting headaches that refused to let up. I glanced at the small mirror on the wall. No matter what, I knew that I wasn't insane. I knew that there was an answer for all of this. I just had to find it. The nurse and the technician were waiting for me when I emerged.

"Good to go, Angela?" The technician seemed very energetic.

"As good as I can be," I replied. I followed the technician into a room with a giant machine and what looked like an exam table below it.

"Angela, MRI stands for Magnetic Resonance Imaging. This device is a powerful magnet. Do you have any jewelry on?"

"No."

"Are you wearing contacts?"

"No."

"Are you claustrophobic?"

"I guess I'll find out." The technician chuckled.

"Okay, well, if you feel uncomfortable, we can reschedule you for an open MRI machine."

"No, I'll be okay," I hoped out loud.

"Alright, I'm going to have you lay face up on the bed. You'll hear a loud thumping noise when the machine turns on. Don't be alarmed; it sounds kind of like dubstep music," she said with a chuckle.

"Okay," I said, laughing back. I laid down on the table as instructed. She placed earplugs in my ears and put a mask over my face that reminded me of Anthony Hopkins in *Silence of the Lambs.*

"This mask is made of magnetic coils to help us get a clear picture of your brain," she explained. Handing me a squeegee bulb, she held up a finger. "Only use this if you need us to stop the scan. As soon as you squeeze it, it will alert me to your discomfort and I will shut the machine down."

As soon as she sent me into the tube, I could feel the sweat my anxiety had produced all over my body. I shut my eyes as tightly as I could and prayed for God to give me peace. There was a sequence of different scans, lasting about four minutes. After it was all over, I took a deep breath, thanked God, and quickly got off of that table. Now, I just had to *wait*. Once I'd gotten dressed again, I found my way out to the waiting room, where Kyle was reading a magazine.

"How did it go?" The concern was evident in his eyes.

"It freaked me out, but it's over now."

"Well, let's go home." He wrapped his arm around me and we walked out toward the parking lot. On the ride home, I was quiet.

"Do you have a headache right now?" Kyle asked.

"Yes, I think the scan made it worse," I admitted.

"Well, hopefully we'll have some answers in the next few days." We stopped to fill my prescription and the first thing I did when I got home was take that Xanax. The last thing I remember, I was laying in our bed with Kyle's arms wrapped around me...

A loud noise jarred me out of a dead sleep. As soon as I opened my eyes, I shielded them from the glare of the bright sun, which was pouring through our bedroom window.

Wow, it's already morning, I thought.

Suddenly, I heard the slam of the front door. Apparently, Kyle was off to work. Still groggy from the Xanax, I rolled over to stretch my legs across the bed and pulled the pillow up under my head. Just as the sound of silence overtook the room, the house phone began to ring. Assuming it was Kyle, needing something he'd forgotten, I jumped up, grabbed my pink robe from the bedpost, and rushed to answer the phone. "Hello?"

"Hello, is this Angela Russo?"

"This is she," I answered, surprised it wasn't Kyle.

"Hi, Angela, this is Dr. Samuel's office. Your results came back and Dr. Samuel would like for you to come by this morning to go over them."

"Wow, that was fast. Sure, I can be there in about an hour."

"Great, we'll see you then." I jumped into the shower, contemplating bothering Kyle at work. I felt okay to drive, even after the Xanax, but I thought it might be nice to have his support. As I finished blow-drying my hair, I decided not to call Kyle.

I wish Denver were here. I mourned the nonexistence of my fictitious friend. And Kaitlin, who actually was real, was my neighbor, but we'd exchanged maybe ten words in the past two years. The thought of striking up a friendship with her seemed unlikely. *How would that conversation go? Hey, Kaitlin, I had a dream that we were friends, but my boyfriend, who also happened to be the Antichrist, blew up your house and killed you.* Yeah, I was on my own.

Finishing up in the bathroom, I walked out to my closet and selected a purple dress off of a hanger. Slipping it over my head, I began to worry. *What if they found a brain tumor? How will I ever be able to tell Kyle?* I put on a pair of lavender flats, grabbed my purse and keys, and headed out my garage door.

Kyle had gotten me a new cell phone, so I made sure I turned it off. I figured it was better for him to think I was still in bed sleeping off the Xanax. When I arrived at Dr. Samuel's office, the same nurse I'd seen the day before greeted me. "Hey, Angela, welcome back. Please sign in here and I'll take you back."

I scrawled my name onto their clipboard, not surprised at my shaking hand. I followed her back immediately, despite the others who were waiting with their magazines. I was puzzled by the fact that we went a different direction down the hall.

"I'm taking you to his office," the nurse explained. My heart instantly began to beat faster. There was definitely a spike in my anxiety. As soon as we walked into the room, my eyes scanned it. A large, cherry wood desk rested on a beautiful, burgundy, rectangular rug. Two tall-backed, leather chairs sat in front of his desk. There were pictures of his family scatter on top of his desk. More diplomas and numerous achievements hung on the walls. "Have a seat Angela and he'll be in shortly."

"Okay." I couldn't even manage a smile. I slid back into one of the chairs. My nerves raged inside me, my mind raced with questions, and my chest dripped with sweat.

When Dr. Samuel entered the room, I noticed my name on the file in his hand. A surreal feeling washed over me. I suddenly felt that my whole life's destiny might be contained in that single file, just inches away from me.

"Good morning, Angela. Did the Xanax help you sleep?"

"Yes, it did. Thank you."

"Great. Well, Angela, once your results came back yesterday, I went over the report with a few of my colleagues. I have to tell you, I am extremely baffled with my findings." *Baffled? That doesn't sound good.* He sat behind his desk, opening my sacred file.

"What do you mean by 'baffled'?" I asked. He stared cautiously into my eyes.

"Angela, the test results came back with something unexplainable showing up in the cervical part of your neck." *Oh. My. God.*

"Dr. Samuel, what is it?" Fear gripped me as I asked a question I already knew the answer to.

"Angela…this may sound strange, but it looks like some sort of an RFID device…" Before he could finish, I pushed back the leather chair and screamed, "Please, God! No! No!"

Suddenly, I felt a sensation as if I were about to faint.

* * * *

185

The next thing I knew, I looked over at my left arm, trying to figure out what was holding me down. As I looked over, I noticed a tattoo on my wrist where a Scripture was written. Proverbs 3:5. *What*? Shaking my head, I shut my eyes and squeeze them even tighter as I tried to focus once again. *Oh no, this can't be*! I franticly looked around the room. *No, No, Please, God No!*

Still overcome by the feeling of grogginess, I struggled to focus once more, telling myself that this can't be real. *Angela, think straight.* I tried to pull up my arm to wipe my eyes as the tears of frustration mingled with the fogginess of confusion, but the pressure of the restraints resisted and became even tighter. The Velcro closure of the cuffs dug into my flesh angrily. That was when I noticed the IV sticking out of my arm. The sight of the IV panicked me more. The tattoo farther down my arm again caught my attention. *No this can't be, I got that tattoo when I was in my forties.*

Off in the distance I could hear footsteps coming closer; I started to panic. As I looked around the room, the familiarity of it made me realize that this was the same room where I was kept tied down after they killed Chase. I was back at Aaron's house. *I thought it was all a dream? Am I going insane? Where's Molly and Ermika? Where is my Mommy?* Lifting my head to listen, suddenly the footsteps stopped and I could hear the creak of door handle turning. Looking toward the door I tried to make out the image walking in. All I could discern was the figure of a man.

"Who is it?" I yelled out. "Kyle? Is it you? Dr. Samuel? Aaron?" I could feel his presence as he walked closer to me. The echo of his footsteps filled the room. I strained to glimpse the man and all I could see were his blue eyes looking at me.

"Angela, Angela shh...lay still it's me Michael Victory, I am going to get you out of here." I felt the restraints start to loosen.

"You need to be quiet Angela while I carry you out of here. If we get caught Aaron will kill us both."

Afraid to make a sound I just laid there, trying to figure out what the hell was going on. He wrapped a white terrycloth housecoat around me as he picked me up in his arms. I went in and out of consciousness and the dizziness made me nauseous as he carried me down a hallway. The dark staircase felt damp from the cold air that rushed in from outside. Fear that mixed with happiness washed through my body. *I am getting out of there!*

"Hold on Angela, while I lay you in the back seat and cover you with this blanket. We need to make it past the guard at the security office." I could feel the cold from the leather seats immediately penetrate my body. Closing my eyes in fear, I tried to relax, but the next thing I knew I was playing outside under an apple tree. Looking up, I saw a lady walking toward me.

"Hi, honey, what is your name?"

"Angela Russo," I answered politely.

"Well, hello, Angela! Would you like to come and play with my little girl? Her name is Tricia. We just moved in down the street.

Is your mommy home? My name is Miss Courtney. How old are you, honey?"

"I'm six and yes, I would love to play with Tricia! I'll go get my mommy!" Jumping up, I ran as fast as I could to our front door. "Mommy! Mommy!" I yelled in excitement.

"Angela? Darling, are you alright?" I heard my mommy's voice coming from the kitchen.

"There is a lady out front. She just moved in down the street. She wants to see you and she wants to know if I can play with her little girl. Her name's Tricia. Can I, Mommy? Please?"

"Hold on, Angela. Calm down," she came around the corner wearing a flower-patterned dress, with her hair swirled up into a bun.

"She's outside waiting, Mommy!" I exclaimed.

"Okay, sweetie, let's go talk to her." As soon as we stepped out onto our front porch, we found Miss Courtney sitting in our rocking chair.

"Miss Courtney, this is my mommy," I said, suddenly feeling shy. Miss Courtney stood to shake my mother's hand. I realized how pretty she was. She had beautiful, long blonde hair, brilliant blue eyes, and slender legs. Her smile was radiant. I wanted my mommy to like her so I could go and play at her house with Tricia.

"Hello, I'm Courtney, your new neighbor. I just moved in a few doors down," she pointed to their house, where a mini-van was parked in the driveway. My mother shook her hand and smiled back.

"Hi Courtney, it's nice to meet you. Welcome to our neighborhood. My name is Isabella Russo."

"Well, Isabella, my daughter, Tricia, is about Angela's age. I would love for them to meet. Tricia has been anxious to make new friends here. Would you mind if Angela came over to play for a few hours?" I couldn't contain my excitement any longer.

"Can I, Mommy? Can I?"

"Okay, honey, but you need to be home for dinner by five."

"Thank you, Mommy!" I relished my victory as I hugged her and ran inside to grab my two favorite dolls, Molly and Ermika. I kissed my mother goodbye and headed down the driveway with Miss Courtney to meet my new friend, Tricia.

Young Innocence

Three driveways down from mine, Miss Courtney and I turned to walk up toward her house. A young girl spotted us from the backyard and hurried down to us. Her long ponytail, which was the same color as Miss Courtney's, waved behind her as she ran. She wore pink shorts that hugged her thin little body and pink sneakers that were laced halfway up with pink and white shoelaces.

"Hello!" she said excitedly. "I'm Tricia!" Her big, green eyes sparkled under thick lashes that batted at us in excitement.

"Hi, Tricia! I'm Angela and I brought some of my dolls to play with."

"Ooooh, come on," she practically squealed as she waved for me to follow her, "I have a dollhouse in my bedroom!"

As soon as I stepped into Courtney and Tricia's house, I felt peace wash over me. Pictures of angels hung on the walls of the short hallway. When Tricia opened the door to her bedroom, the first thing I noticed was the white clouds painted on the sky blue walls of her tiny bedroom. In the corner, I saw her huge dollhouse with little doll furniture and frilly decor inside. A pink and white flowered comforter snugged her canopy bed that sat in the middle of the room, scattered with stuffed animals perched on top. I knew instantly that Tricia and I were going to be friends for a long time. And while I played with Tricia, none of the memories of Lucifer touching my body entered my mind.

Hours passed quickly when Tricia and I played together. We would sit under her big weeping willow tree in their backyard, giggling breathlessly all afternoon. I loved listening to the Bible stories she had learned from her mother. One afternoon, she looked straight into my eyes and asked, "Angela, do you want Jesus to live in your heart?"

I looked at her, confused, without knowing what to say. I got up and began to pace back and forth in the grass. Maybe it was time to tell Tricia that I was a princess. *Don't you dare*, a deep voice hissed in my head. My thoughts scattered as I realized it was *his* voice. He had told me that I could only belong to him, so I couldn't have Jesus live in my heart.

"I can't," I whispered just above a breath. "He won't let me." Now Tricia was confused.

"Who won't let you, Angela?"

"Him...I...I can't talk about it." I looked away from her eyes, hating that I couldn't tell my friend the secret I had also been keeping from my mother.

"What can't you talk about?" Tricia asked, not willing to let the matter go.

"Nothing," I snapped. "Just nothing!" My eyes darted back toward her, and then quickly away again.

"Angela, you know that Jesus loves you? My mommy says that He is stronger than anyone in this whole wide world. His daddy is God, who *made* the world." Her words burned in my soul. I wanted so badly to be protected from that voice and the eyes that filled my nightmares. If Jesus could protect me, then…*no*. I was Lucifer's princess. He had claimed my soul and my body. Jesus wasn't allowed to have me.

"Maybe tomorrow, Tricia. I have to go home now." I plucked my dolls out of the grass beside us, tucked them under my arm, and hurried down the driveway. "See you tomorrow, Tricia!" I called behind me, not wanting her to be upset with me.

I wondered if I should go to Mr. Ralph's house and talk to him. Maybe he could reassure me. Maybe he would even say that it was okay to have Jesus in my heart. But then, I realized that if Jesus could keep me from Lucifer, then Mr. Ralph might get mad at me for wanting Jesus in my heart. He might even tell me I couldn't play with Tricia anymore. Scary thoughts ran through my mind, *"Like wild horses in a field,"* as my mommy would say.

Instead of Mr. Ralph's house, I began walking toward my own house. As soon as I walked in the door, I heard my mother's voice from the kitchen.

"Angela? Angela, is that you, honey?"

"Yes, Mommy. It's me."

"Why are you home so early, sweetie? Everything okay?" *Think fast, Angela.*

"Umm, because my belly was hurting, Mommy." She walked toward me, placing a hand on my forehead.

"Do you feel sick? Or are you maybe just hungry?"

"I'm hungry," I said, breathing in the oregano in the air. I knew from the smell that Mommy was making her special, homemade pizza. As I got closer, the sweet scent of basil made my mouth water.

"Okay, Angela, the pizza will be done soon. I'm sure you'll feel as good as new once you've had some."

"I bet I will, Mommy. I'm going to play in my bedroom with Molly until it's ready. Will you just call me?" She peeked around the corner to smile at me.

"I sure will, sweetheart." Her smile wasn't as bright as it had once been, but it still made me smile, even with all of the uncertainty I felt.

There were no pictures of angels hanging in the walls of our hallway, but there were old pictures of when life was happier, when Daddy was alive and Mommy had no worries. I opened my bedroom door. *My safe place.* The yellowing walls reflected the sunlight, making them glisten and sparkle when the rays streamed through my sheer, white curtains. I didn't have clouds, like Tricia did, but I had pictures of sunflowers. My twin-size bed, with its green and yellow fluffy pillows, was pushed against my bedroom wall, giving me plenty of room to play on my big, brown oval rug that covered the hardwood floor.

"We're home, Molly," I said cheerfully, pulling her out from underneath my arm. Molly was my very favorite doll. I loved talking to her, and swirling her long brown pigtails around my fingertips. She was the only one I could share my secret with. I made her sit and listen intently as I rambled on about what had happened on that strange afternoon with Mr. Ralph. Staring into her unblinking brown eyes, I told her how frightened I was when Lucifer's hand was under my dress and when I saw the blood on his hands afterward. I knew Molly wasn't real, but telling her the truth made me feel safe. And for now, I didn't have to guard the secret all by myself. Now, Molly would help me keep it.

Liven My Soul

As always, Mommy's pizza was scrumptious. The hot, greasy oil dripped through the buttery crust and onto my hands. Looking up, I realized my mother was staring at me, but she seemed to be deep in thought. It was as though she was staring straight *through* me. I stared back until she blinked and then took a sip from her wine glass. Suddenly, I watched tears gather in her eyes and I wondered what she was thinking. I quickly grabbed the white paper napkin from beside my plate, wiped the oil from my hands, and hurried over to rub her back.

"Are you okay, Mommy?" She placed her hand over the top of mine on her shoulder.

"Yes, honey, I was just thinking about how your daddy is missing pizza night."

I never understood why God had taken my daddy away, but I knew Mommy was mad at God for it. Before Daddy had died, we all went to church every Sunday. But once he was gone, Mommy didn't want to go back. The last day I had set foot in a church was the day of my baptism.

*My baptism...*I remembered that day very well. I remembered thinking I looked as beautiful as brides did on their wedding day. And I remembered Daddy explaining to me that I was getting baptized to give my soul to Jesus. So, how could Lucifer say I was his if I had already given my soul to Jesus? I decided that I would much rather belong to Jesus. When I heard stories about Him, I felt peace, the way I felt when I walked down Tricia's hallway and saw the angels on the wall. Lucifer only frightened me. I wanted desperately to tell Tricia about what had happened that afternoon with my godfather, but I had promised I wouldn't tell anyone. I just had to keep silent about it. Mommy looked at me through her tears.

"I am so sorry for crying in front of you, honey. I just miss your daddy so much."

"I know, Mommy," I said, hugging her. "I miss him, too." *If only she knew that I will be a Queen soon...that would make everything okay.* But Molly was the only one I could tell.

"Angela, you need to take your bath before you go to bed tonight. Go play for a bit and I will call you when your bath is ready."

"Okay, Mommy," I said obediently, and hurried down the hall to resume playing with Molly. I found her where I had left her, sitting on my bed next to Ermika.

"Hi, Molly! Hi, Ermika!" I greeted them. "Did you miss me? You missed out on pizza! And I missed you!" I lowered my voice as I confided in them about what had happened at dinner. "My mommy was crying again tonight. I wish I could tell her about me being a future Queen. Oh, Molly…" I snatched her off of the bed. "I sure do like my new friend, Tricia. How about you? And how about you, Ermika?" Ermika stared at me from the bed in response. "Maybe we will go play with her again after school tomorrow." A few minutes later, I heard my mommy's voice coming down the hall.

"Angela, your bath is ready. Come on, honey!"

"Okay, Mommy. Be right there!" Placing Molly back on the bed, I skipped over to my dresser and pulled a pair of my pink princess pajamas out of a drawer, along with my pink princess slippers. Taking one last glance at Molly and Ermika, I said, "See you in a few minutes! Coming, Mommy," I said as I hurried down the hallway where my mother was waiting for me.

"Angela, jump in and make sure you wash your hair. Rinse the shampoo out really well, okay?"

"Okay, Mommy," I promised as she disappeared back down the hall. I splashed the bubbles around in whirls with my hands and dunked my head into the water. I squeezed the strawberry shampoo out into my hand and rubbed it onto my head, shutting my eyes tightly to keep them from burning. Once I had rinsed it out of my hair, I used my washcloth to clean my body. The water began to cool off and I decided I didn't want to stay in as long as I usually did. After climbing out, drying off, and putting my pajamas on, I called to her, "All clean, Mommy!"

"Okay, brush your teeth and I will come tuck you in."

"Alright," I tried to keep the grumble out of my voice. I hated brushing my teeth. Once I'd finished, I walked down the hall and crawled into my bed, placing Molly on one side of me and Ermika on the other, before pulling the covers over us.

"Are you in bed, Angela?" I heard Mommy call.

"Yes, Mommy! I am." Seconds later, the door opened and she walked in, leaving the door open behind her just a crack. The tears had been replaced with a smile.

"Honey, I want you to know that I love you very much," she whispered, leaning down to kiss my forehead. "Sweet dreams, Angela."

"Goodnight, Mommy. I love you, too."

"Goodnight, Molly. Goodnight, Ermika. Have sweet dreams, girls," Mommy said as she shut the lights off and left the room. With the lights off, I felt fear creep in as it always did. But I remembered what Tricia had told me. Jesus could protect me.

As quietly as I could, I slipped out of bed and got onto my knees, the way they had taught me in Sunday school. Shutting my eyes, I whispered, "Jesus, I don't know if you can hear me, but if you can, I am a little bit confused right now. I really want you to come into my heart. But, Lucifer said that I am his and no one else can have me. Can you help me understand what's going on? Can you keep me safe? And, can you make my mommy happy again? Amen."

I opened my eyes and suddenly I felt embarrassed. I was only asking for things, which wasn't polite. Closing my eyes again, I added, "By the way, thank you for my friend, Tricia. I really like her.

Thank you, Jesus, and goodnight. Amen." Hopping back into bed, I pulled the covers over my head.

The Dream

With Molly under my right arm and Ermika under my left, I watched the glow of the full moon coming through my window. The soft rays illuminated Ermika's face, making her skin look even darker than it really was. When I closed my eyes, the pictures of my family that line our hallway danced in my mind. Every muscle in my body started to relax. Tranquility flooded over me and I drifted off into a sweet, deep sleep.

The next thing I knew, I was standing on top of a mountain, surrounded by bright, green fields. Ahead of me, three deer overlooked the mountain. As I approached the edge, I noticed a cloud-like mist coming down out of the atmosphere, blanketing a beautiful, round shape that resembled pictures I'd seen of the Earth. As I stared into the distance, a soft voice spoke to me. It asked a question: "Angela, are you looking at what lies ahead of you?"

"Yes, I am," I replied, as though it was perfectly normal to respond to an invisible voice.

"What do you see?"

"I see the world."

"And what else?"

"A beautiful ocean, with mist falling from the sky."

"Do you know what this means, Angela?"

"No, but it's beautiful."

"My love is like a mist. It comes down from Heaven and covers the world. I make everything beautiful and when you are with me, there is no fear. Only peace. Look to your side. What do you see, Angela?" I turned and realized the three little deer were walking toward me.

"Three little deer."

"Are you afraid of those deer, Angela?" I laughed, delighted.

"No, of course not! How could I ever be afraid of something so cute, like these three little innocent creatures?" I took a step toward them and when I felt the cool grass beneath my feet, I realized I was barefoot. The deer began to nibble at the grass next to my feet. They didn't seem frightened by my presence either. My smile grew wide as I studied their fuzzy, brown hair and their white, fluffy tails. Once again, the voice spoke to me, and when the voice spoke, I felt a cool sensation mixed with a warm breeze blowing through my hair, as if someone was breathing on me. It made me feel alive.

"Do you fear *Me*, Angela?"

"No, not at all," I replied.

"Do you know who I am?"

"Yes, you are God. You created the Universe."

"Yes, Angela, I am the Creator of the Universe. I created you before you were even born. I was the one who picked your mother and father to bring you into this World." Sadness washed over me when I thought about my father dying, leaving my mother to take care of us all by herself. I knew that God did always provide for us; we never went without. There was always food on the table and clothes on our backs. I knew I should be thankful, but I missed my daddy, and I couldn't understand why we had to experience the pain of his death.

"Angela, from your perspective, it is hard for you to understand certain things. You must remember, everyone and everything I have created is on Earth to fulfill a specific purpose. You are a traveler passing through, just like your mother and just like your father. You must come to understand that Earth is not your real home. Then, and only then, will you recognize your true purpose.

"Once this happens, the entire picture will be revealed, instead of just pieces of a puzzle. You will know the meaning of life and your existence. Nothing will be able to stop you; nothing will stand in your way. You will fulfill your mission here on Earth."

I nodded, but the image of Lucifer crept into my mind. "Remember, I am the Creator of all things. I give life and I take life. I am the source of Life. So, do not fear Lucifer. Your soul does not belong to him, Angela. You belong to Me and you always have. You are My little girl. My Princess. Lucifer wants you because he knows how important you are to Me. But he also knows that *with* Me, you are untouchable, so he will try to sway you from the knowledge that you are Mine. During these times, listen for My voice, Angela. I will be cheering you on as you complete your mission. My protection is on you. Follow Me closely and I will guide your every step." There was something I never understood and although I was talking with the Creator, I felt bold enough to ask.

"If you are God, wasn't it You who created Lucifer?"

"Yes, Lucifer is a part of my creation, but he chose to go against the laws I created for the Universe."

"Why did you allow him to?" I stood with my arms crossed, like a pretentious child.

"If I didn't listen to my mommy when she makes rules, she would ground me." The voice chuckled at my childish reasoning.

"I grounded him for *many* years, Angela. But like all of my creation, I gave him the gift of free will. I will always love him because I created him. But his pride led him to believe that he knew better than Me.

"Pride deceives the proud into believing it lifts them up, but it serves only to put them down. Pride has been Lucifer's downfall, but Lucifer has a choice. He can either obey Me and the laws I've created, or he will suffer consequences in the end."

At least it was good to know that someday he would be punished for what he had done. "My Sweet Angela, my ways might seem difficult at times, but I promise I will be with you. Always remember: no weapon formed against you shall ever prosper when you stand for Me. I will give you peace and strength. Seek Me and you shall find Me and your hindrances shall be few."

I felt myself suddenly traveling backwards. The speed was so great that I could see my hair flying out in front of me. Memories and thoughts flashed in my mind like fireworks exploding in a grand finale. Then, I heard my mother's voice…

"Angela, it's time to get up for school. Come on, Angela! Let's go, honey. You're running late." I laid in my bed for a moment, trying to figure out what had just happened.

"Wow, that was a dream," I muttered in Molly's direction.

"Are you okay, Angela?" Mommy asked. "Are you feeling sick?" I looked up at my mother's concerned expression.

"No, Mommy, I'm fine. I just had a dream that felt very real."

"What was it, honey?"

"Hmmm…I can't remember now," I said, sheepishly. But I did remember. I remembered every single detail of that dream. I just didn't want to share it with her. She wouldn't understand. It had to be just another secret I kept from her. Only Molly and Ermika could hear the details. Mommy laughed.

"Okay, sweetie. Well, hurry up and get dressed. I need to get you to school before you're late!"

"I'll hurry, Mommy," I promised. Jumping out of my bed, I quickly slipped into my white sundress and a yellow sweater. I skipped down the hallway, brushed my teeth, washed my face, and pulled my hair up into a ponytail with my white scrunchie.

"I'm ready, Mommy!" I called. I shut off the light in the bathroom and skipped back down the hall to my bedroom. I stuck my head in the door and told Molly and Ermika, "See you later! Off to school I go…but when I'm back, I have so much to tell you both!"

Paradise

"Angela, you okay back there? They've been giving you Rohypnol to keep you unconscious until Aaron returns from Rome. I've called your son, Nicholas, to let him know that I've got you and you're safe. Angela, can you hear me? You're safe now. Everything is going to be okay." I could hear a man's voice fading in and out as I tried to focus on what he was saying. *Nick is my son, but I was just with my mother. Is this a dream? I don't know what's real anymore. What is going on? Why can't I focus?* Feeling cold I pulled the blanket that covered me closer to my face.

I finally responded, "Where have I been? And who are you?"

"Angela, my name is Michael Victory. I went to school with your son, Nicholas. I was hired as one of Aaron Stone's bodyguards when he was in Nashville. I received training from BUD/S and served as a United States Naval Special Warfare Commander. Trust me, you are safe with me." A cloudy memory came back to me. It was of me talking to Nick through a game on my phone. I had heard the name Michael Victory. I knew at once that I really could entrust my safety to him.

"How long were you a Navy Seal?"

"Over eleven years."

"Michael, where are you taking me?"

"We're going to New Jersey. We're going to meet Nicholas and Denver." I couldn't believe my ears. *DENVER? Oh my God she's still alive.*

"Denver is alive?"

"Yes, she is. When she was on the phone with you, just before the explosion, do you remember hearing her scream?"

"Yes, I remember," I said, chills running down my spine at the recollection.

"I was there, Angela. I didn't have time to explain what was happening. I took the phone away and got her out of the house just before it exploded. As quickly as I could, I hid her and I had to wait to tell Nicholas where she was until after we were certain we could find you." He caught my eye in the rearview mirror. "Angela, we're running out of time. The Pope gave his resignation yesterday. This is the first papal resignation in almost six hundred years. Just hours after his announcement, lightning hit St. Peter's dome at the Vatican. I believe it is God's way of reassuring His people that no matter what, He is still in control of the world. The Pope will step down and Prophesy will take over, Angela. Pope Petrus will be the last pope to usher in the Messiah, or, as we know him, the Antichrist. Aaron will rise to power within a few short weeks."

"Do you know my other two sons Michael? Mario and Dante?"

"Yes, Angela, I do. They're out of harm's way."

"I need to get in touch with them immediately, to let them know I'm okay. And it's time they knew the truth about what is in store in the next few weeks."

"Nicholas has filled them in," Michael assured me. I sighed.

"Thank God," I said in relief. Letting my head fall to rest on the back seat, I wondered what had happened to Kyle. But still, the love I'd once felt for Aaron was a bittersweet memory. A part of me wanted to shout for Michael Victory to stop the car, turn around, and go back to Aaron. Another part of me wanted to see Aaron again, to confront him, and ask him how he could do the things he had when I had loved him so much.

I could feel the heat from the SUV's engine blowing warm air through the vents onto my face as I lay there reminiscing about things Aaron and I use to do. In spite of the fact that I feared our future together, he somehow still had a soft spot in my heart. I asked myself the same question over and over. *If we were supposed to be with each other, is this then a divinely orchestrated force holding us together? Is our future destiny in the hands of our Creator?*

The sound of a helicopter racing above the car permeated my thoughts. I sat up, throwing the blanket off me and looked out the back window. I saw his face through the passenger side window of the helicopter—it was Aaron. The moment I saw his face, my heart melted. Even though I was running from him, my emotions swept over me and I wanted to run *toward* him.

I screamed out to Michael, "It's Aaron! It's Aaron! He's in the helicopter! I see his face! He's going to kill us, Michael! He is never going to let me go!" Michael pushed the gas pedal and the SUV lurched.

He yelled, "Pray, Angela! I've got to get you out of here safely!"

I called out, "God, if you're there, please help us. I belong to you, not Lucifer."

Suddenly, my senses were cut off as everything went dark. We were driving through some sort of tunnel. The sound of the helicopter faded away into the distance.

"Thank you, God!" I cried.

But fear gripped me as I realized that Aaron would be at the end of the tunnel, waiting for me with his helicopter. Michael slammed on the breaks. The car screeched to a stop and Michael turned the car around. We now faced the way we came in. Luckily, there hadn't been any other cars in the tunnel and we raced back toward the entrance. As he pulled out of the tunnel, Michael barked instructions, "Get out Angela! Grab your phone from underneath the seat!" I was shocked to see that it was still there, but I guess Michael had charged it and put it back, knowing I might need it in the future.

Michael told me to wait for him. If he didn't come back for me, I was to find a ride to the Port Authority in Newark, where I would meet Denver and Nick at Maher Terminal. Once we got to the ship, we were supposed to walk up the gangplank and use his name with the blond guard, Brandon, to gain passage on the ship.

I threw off the blanket, slipped out of terrycloth robe that was covering my clothes, grabbed my phone, and ran to the side of the road. I stumbled my way over a railing and rolled into the gully beside it. The sound of the helicopter propellers rushed over my head, sending shivers down my spine that had nothing to do with the cold weather. I didn't know how long I lay there, wishing the helicopter would pass. It felt like hours. When it finally did, I crawled to the side of the road and managed to lift myself up over the railing. There was no sign of Michael Victory.

Once out on the road again, I began walking, turning back every few minutes to keep an eye out for Michael Victory. Eventually, I lost sight of the tunnel completely. I realized he probably wasn't coming back.

Traffic on the road was light. A beige SUV had passed on the opposite side of the road, but I refused to make eye contact with the driver, in case it was Aaron's men looking for me. Luckily, they passed by without even slowing down. Several minutes later, I heard the engine of a sports car. I flagged it down. The woman who drove the cute, little, red sports car climbed out to help me get in.

"Hi, my name is Angela. My car broke down and I was on my way to meet my son at the Port Authority."

The woman smiled in response. "Hi, I am Rhonda. The funny thing is, I'm heading there myself. I work for Customs and Border Protection and my office is there."

After climbing into Rhonda's car, I shut my eyes and leaned my head back. *Thank you, God! I know You are in control.* We made small talk about our children as Rhonda and I drove along. When we arrived at Port Authority, she dropped me at the front gate. I looked into her eyes. "Thank you so much, Rhonda," I said, with sincerity in my voice, trying to suppress the fear that I felt deep in my soul. *Did Michael Victory make it safely? Are Denver and Nick going to be there waiting for me?* As I climbed out of the car, the brisk, cold air took away my breath. I ran in through the sliding doors.

The moment I was inside, I turned right down a white, tiled hallway. The Port Authority police covered every exit. Fearing that they worked for Aaron, I kept my head down. Overhead, there were signs directing me to the Maher Terminal. I slipped into the bathroom to wash my face and braid my hair so I didn't look so obvious.

As I was walking out the door, I glanced to the right and saw a man heading toward me. His red eyes were glowing. I instinctively turned around and went back into the ladies' room until he passed. Peeking out the door again, I slid out of the doorway and down the hall toward Maher Terminal.

When I approached the gates, I could see them. Nicholas and Denver stood there with Mario, Dante, and Beau. Tears streamed down my cheeks when I saw my children. I thought to myself, *we made it! They are all alive!* The feeling of joy overwhelmed me as Denver ran toward me and threw her arms around me. I took a step back and studied their faces. "Have you heard from Michael?"

Nicholas and Beau exchanged glances. "Not yet, Ma." We quickly headed down the stairs and through a door that led outside to the docks. The enormous ship had its gangplank down, yet was deserted, save for a lone man at the top. As our group reached him, I spoke first.

"Are you Brandon? Michael Victory sent us to you."

He smiled at me and said, "Aye, welcome." Brandon motioned for us to follow him. He led us into a room deep in the bowels of the ship. We looked around the room, noticing six cots all lined up against the walls.

For the first time in days, maybe weeks, I felt safe. Surrounded by the people I loved, I was filled with gratitude. I thought back to that dream I had as a little girl where God told me I belonged to Him and not to Lucifer. I thanked Him for rescuing me. Brandon surveyed our anxious faces and said, "All aboard. Next stop, Paradise."

The End

And now, a sneak preview of the second installment of the Aaron Stone Trilogy (coming soon):

Aaron Stone: Lost in Shangri-La

Preface

The future is upon us. Somehow, I have found myself playing a very important role in the New World Order. Totalitarianism, a political system in which the state holds total authority over society and seeks to control all aspects of our public and private lives, is threatening to overtake the whole world. No one will be safe from Aaron Stone. If Aaron rises up, he will control the thoughts and action of every single citizen. As Aaron the Dictator, the charismatic, cult-driven aspect of his personality will prevail. It will assist him in using mass media and propaganda to shape himself into a god-like image.

He will be set apart and treated as supernatural and superhuman. Aaron plans to demonstrate his extraordinary insight, which will naturally inspire loyalty and obedience from his followers. His New World order will come from a secretive power of elites, with a globalist agenda, conspiring to rule the world. This secret political assembly has already decided to make Aaron's body a vessel. He will host a combined life force by way of an injection of Triple helix and other DNA strands. Having these inter-dimensional deities inside Aaron will allow said elite figures to control Aaron.

Aaron Stone: Dancing with the Devil

The new-and-improved Aaron, the New World Order leader, can arise now that Pope Benedict XVI has resigned his papal office. In the Christian world, Aaron will be known as the Anti-Christ who will come on the scene when the rest of the world leaders have failed. His alien bloodline will give him the knowledge to act and become like the Jewish messiah that the world has been waiting for.

What is my role in this elaborate, evil scheme, you may ask? An ordinary woman, a divorced, devout, mother of three grown sons? Well, for starters, two essential things are holding Aaron back—God's Spirit and my love. Aaron needs me by his side to fulfill his mission. I was chosen from birth to be linked with Aaron—or should I say that I am to be linked with the one who will eventually take over his spirit—Lucifer himself. So as long as I am on the run, Lucifer's reign will have to be postponed. If Aaron can't find me, he can't take over the world.